true love

AND OTHER DREAMS OF MIRACULOUS ESCAPE

micah perks

Outpost19 | San Francisco
outpost19.com

Perks, Micah
        True Love and Other Dreams of Miraculous
Escape/ Micah Perks
        ISBN: 9781944853556 (pbk)

OUTPOST19

ORIGINAL
PROVOCATIVE
READING

true love

AND OTHER DREAMS OF MIRACULOUS ESCAPE

micah perks

For my children,
magical unbalancers,
beloved unhingers,
the ones who make
a difference

"My life has not turned out as I expected"

- Harry Houdini

Table of Contents

King of Chains

Chain, chain, chain, chain, chain, chain
Chain, chain, chain, chain of fools
—Aretha Franklin

Hold your breath, and you will observe such wonders! Mercurial escapes, absurd and endless construction, utopian dreams, outrageous savagery, the whole shebang, but let me begin at the beginning. In 1915, I was covering the San Francisco World's Fair for *The Examiner*, my first full-time job as a reporter. We'd been rocked and almost wrecked in 1906, so this celebration showed the world that everything in Frisco was copacetic again. I covered the fair right from the beginning, with headlines like, "Wonder of Wonders" and "Heady Times These." Alexander Graham Bell placed a cross-country phone call, Thomas Edison showed off his storage battery, Henry Ford created an automobile extravaganza. General Electric covered the exhibition in tiny lights—even the boats in the harbor twinkled. The centerpiece of the whole mishegas was the Tower of Jewels. One of my stories detailed the 102,000 pieces of glittering multicolored cut Bohemian glass used in construction.

The World's Fair was the bee's knees, as we used to say, but by November the fair was winding down, and I was having to do a little digging to make my weekly deadline.

I reread the official brochure, and the last paragraph caught my eye: "Do you realize what this Exposition means to you? This is the first time in the history of man the entire world is known and in intercommunication. In speaking of the earth, the qualification 'The *known* world' is no longer necessary."

I was a man of knowledge myself, a member of the Socialist Party, voted for Eugene Debs, read Upton Sinclair. We believed the truth would set us free. But all the world could not be known quite yet—why then pursue knowledge? Plus, I'd be out of a job. Although so far I'd only written about the Exposition, I wanted to be a muckraker like Fremont Older, eradicating humbug and skullduggery. I searched about for some unexplored murky corner of the Great Exposition to shine my light on. And that's when Houdini came to town.

The King of Chains, the World Famous Self-liberator, the Elusive American, the Prince of the Air, the Handcuff King, the Jail Breaker. He was a foreigner, and everyone loved him as if he were Yankee Doodle. First, he escaped Hungary, and then (perhaps even harder) he escaped Appleton, Wisconsin. His father was a rabbi, but he seemed to have liberated himself from our religion, too. And though he himself was a master of illusion, he worked to unmask the quacksters. He'd even written a book exposing the flimflam of the underworld. Why, he was our national inspiration.

I went to his show at the Orpheum. His dark hair was greased down and parted in the middle, his eyes made up like Sarah Bernhardt. He never smiled on stage, so he appeared to be glowering, in possession of mysteries the audience could not fathom. "Welcome, Friends," he began. His voice was deep and sounded slightly British. He hit those fricatives hard. His accent was just another thing he'd escaped.

He performed his world famous Chinese Water Torture Cell Escape. It was a doozy, fully copyrighted, though I'm not sure what was Chinese about it. His feet were locked into what appeared to be a lid for a great tank of water. The sides of the tank were glass plated, and inside was a metal cage. They lowered him upside down into the cage inside the tank. Then they locked the lid. His assistant stood by with a sledgehammer in case he had to break in to save him from drowning. The curtains closed.

The seconds ticked. The audience murmured nervously. I sat in my velvet-covered seat, holding my own breath and thinking about how I was like Houdini—like him, I'd tried to erase my foreign accent, never went to shul, was taken for a real American. But I was also not like Houdini. I was twenty-five and still lived with my mother and sister. I had wanted to ride a motorbike across America that next summer, send articles from the road, but my mother had forbidden it—too dangerous, she said.

I gasped. I couldn't hold my breath like Houdini, either. I imagined the Great Escape from the Mother Embrace. A mother standing behind the King of Chains, her arms straitjacketing him, Houdini dislocating his own shoulders to free himself. And then I heard the applause start, looked up and there he was, Houdini, bouncing around in front of the curtain, a free man.

At that very moment the idea came to me, like one of Mr. Ford's motorcars straight off the assembly line, audacious and gleaming.

When I went backstage to interview Houdini, he was in a heavy floor-length maroon satin robe, untied. Underneath, he still wore his black bathing costume. His legs were hairless and extraordinarily developed. His muscular chest was also shaved, but his forearms gave him away as one of us—they were covered in wiry black hair just like my own. He was wiping off his eye make-up, which appeared to be grease paint from the circus. In posters and even on stage his eyes looked almost black, but up close they were maybe what you call hazel—green with an explosion of gold in the middle. His springy hair was already curling out of the brilliantine. He was a good-looking fellow, if you like the foreigner type, and I hope you do. He sort of hopped on his toes all the time, as if he had so much energy wound up he needed to continually let it out in those little hops. Some say the secret to his success was that he was double-jointed, but I think it was that energy—he was a twentieth century dynamo.

When he finished cleaning his face, he pulled an apple out of the pocket of his dressing gown, began tossing it from hand to hand. His eyes crinkled, and he gave me an easy, pleased-with-itself grin—he had a space between his front teeth. "What can I do you for, Bub?" he asked.

"Albert Tannenbaum with *The Examiner.*" My own hands were clenched inside my pockets, something I'd trained myself to do so I didn't gesture so much. After telling him his show was hunky-dory, I got straight down to business. I pulled him aside and unfolded my scheme. "Say, Mr. Houdini," I began. In a town called San Jose, just a few hours distance from San Francisco, lived the old widow of the Winchester fortune. For twenty-nine years she had been constantly building a house of crazy proportions, supposedly directed by ghosts.

Even from the outside you could tell something was strange. There were thirteen stained glass windows that had thirteen panels fashioned in the shape of spider webs. But no one except the servants could get into that house. They say the front door had never been unlocked. This house was the ultimate unknown. No one but the Great Houdini could break in and shine a bright light on the hokum that surrounded it.

At first when I told him the scheme, he grinned his amused grin, said in his radio voice, "I'm an escapologist, Bub, not a thief. It wouldn't do for me to be caught breaking into someone's home, especially a swank widow's place. Why, I've written a book exposing the tricks of thieves. How would it do if I were marked as one myself? Why don't I just call?" He hopped a bit on his toes, tossed his apple. "I'm sure the old bird would be amused by a visit from Harry Houdini."

I nixed that. I told him that Teddy Roosevelt himself had come to call and was sent away in a huff. While I talked, he caught his apple in his mouth and began eating it. I told him I thought we could get worldwide coverage with a story like this. I knew publicity was Houdini's bread and butter. In my enthusiasm I let my hands fly, outlined the headlines in the air: "'The King Of Chains Reveals Spirit House Is A Sham!' The world needs to know," I added.

He seemed to consider, munching thoughtfully. He said, "You say she is in communication with the dead?"

I winked. "That's what they say."

He tossed me the skinny core of the apple, sloughed off his dressing gown and flipped into a handstand right in front of me. I looked down at him grinning up at me. "Is that a yes?" I asked, and he nodded. I slipped the core into my pocket, a souvenir.

Two days later, his assistant dropped off a heavy silver milk can in front of the service entrance of the Winchester Spirit House. After thirteen minutes in the late afternoon sun, servants came out of the house, heaved up the can, grumbling to each other, hauled it inside, and there was Houdini, up to his neck in dairy inside the Winchester mansion.

I'd suggested we use water, but Houdini said milk was a more commodious solution. Sounds echoed strangely in the can. But finally, for seven minutes after he had been carried into the house he heard nothing at all. Houdini was an expert at keeping time, an essential element of his act, as he later told me.

He popped the locked lid off, don't ask me how. It fell onto the floor with a clang. He peeped up over the metal lip, his hair dripping milk. A screech startled him. A red-faced woman in a big food-splattered apron brandishing a wooden spoon locked her predatory eyes with his for six seconds. Houdini was certain she had done the same with many hapless rats before him. Then she bum-rushed him. She sat down on the top of the can, trapping Houdini inside.

He heard the woman, who had an Irish accent, yell,

"I've scared up a bogey in the milk." Then there were a lot of voices. Someone clanged the side of the can, which hurt Houdini's ears. She ordered some so-and-so named Lacy to fetch Mrs. Winchester. The cook announced loudly that the bogey was a dark devil from the Negro or Arab races. A man's voice said, "Could be a genie that grants wishes." The cook repeated that Lacy had gone to alert Mrs. Winchester. "I'm sure she already knows," someone else said, and they all quieted down.

I must admit that at this juncture the Great Houdini wanted out of the adventure. He was soggy. He was hungry, as usual. Even more so, he sensed this scheme turning south—he knew what happened to intruders of the so-called darker races. "Meshuganeh kup, that shyster Albert, what a donkey's ass," he cursed me in both Yiddish and English.

"It's speaking!" someone said.

"What language is that?"

"Arabian." And there were general knockings on the can. For some reason, this tickled Houdini's funny bone. He laughed and knocked back, then philosophically lapped up some of the milk he was bathing in.

Finally, after six more minutes, Houdini had enough. He positioned his palms on the considerable bottom. "It's pinching me, it is!" the cook squealed. Houdini began to lift. There were some appreciative oohs and aahs as Houdini stood, shaking just a little, milk cascading off him, the squeeling cook raised above his head. Even while she battered him about the head and shoulders with the wooden spoon, he said, "Allow me to introduce myself. I am Harry Houdini."

The pummeling ceased. He was surrounded by a

group of servants: the young woman Lacy, pointing a broom at him, two gardeners, one with a rake and another with a trowel, and a well-dressed old butler hefting a paper weight with a scene of the Alps as his weapon.

"That is the great magician himself. I've seen pictures," said Lacy, lowering her broom.

"Ask him if he grants wishes," said the man with the rake. "If we was to rub his tummy like."

Then a haughty voice spoke from behind them, "Kindly lower my cook, Mr. Houdini."

Houdini brought the beefy woman back to earth. She straightened out her dress and apron, her cheeks aflame.

Free of the weight of the cook, Houdini bowed to an extremely short, veiled woman in a dark hobble dress. She looked like a well-appointed dwarf, thick like that, which made Houdini feel at home as he'd had several dwarf colleagues when he worked at the Welsh Brothers Circus.

"What is the meaning of this intrusion?" the Widow Winchester asked.

"I've come to offer my assistance in your battle with the spirits, Madam."

"Please escort Mr. Houdini out." And the snooty, miniature widow turned away.

The old butler holding the paperweight stepped forward. "Mr. Houdini, it would be my privilege—"

"Please, wait, Madam Winchester, I implore you," cried Houdini. "Perhaps it is not you that needs help, but I. I am desperate to contact my dear, darling mother. I am dying with missing her. I never got to say good-bye."

When Houdini told me this story, he was sitting on a green settee in front of a fire in his hotel room on the afternoon after the incident. He was in white silk pajamas eating a Jewish dish he'd asked the kitchen to prepare specially—sour cream with raw vegetables—Farmer's Chop Suey. I was perched on an arm of the settee taking notes. When he told me what he'd said about his mother, I grinned, "Quick thinking, Mr. Houdini. Did the widow buy it?"

He ignored me, continued to narrate in his deep radio voice between bites. I figured he did not care for interruption, and I tried to keep my mouth shut after that.

Mrs. Winchester looked up at him carefully through the veil. Then she had the butler take him away to be cleaned up in her indoor shower.

For some reason, the only attire they offered him was a Japanese kimono, obviously Mrs. Winchester's, pink silk with a red dragon, very wide, but only reaching to his knees and elbows. He did not like to complain.

Then he was fed. Houdini sat in the kitchen in his kimono, Lacy and the cook waiting on him. He said that besides the roast, there was beef soup with dumplings, caviar and shrimps, which he declined due to his Jewish persuasion, then celery flan and orange fool for dessert. He praised each dish lavishly, and by the orange fool, the cook forgave him for hoisting her by her generous petard. She brought over a pot and three cups, and she, Lacy and the Great Houdini took tea together.

Lacy remarked that she was going to search out other employment. The money wasn't worth it, she said, if her nerves were ruined. She couldn't go about her job expecting a devil to pop out of a milk can or a phantom foot to emerge from the toilet and kick her in the arse.

"Don't be a fool," the cook said. "That warn't no devil, it were Mr. Harry Houdini himself, so you'll be telling your grandchildren. And you make double the money here cash every day, so lamp along with you."

Houdini inquired about the origin of the spirit problem in the house. The cook leaned in, whispered, "She's most likely listening, she is, but since she let you stay, she wouldn't mind me telling you that way back when she were a girl in far-off New England, she married the Winchester heir, had a baby girl, and then husband and wee babe both upped and died on her, all mysterious it was. A spiritualist told her that her family be cursed by all the dead of the Winchester rifle, and if she didn't commence to building a house right aways, she were done for. In short, if she stops building, the spirits will kill her. And that's all I'll say on that subject."

On they chatted cheerfully—they trying to get him to reveal the secrets of his escapes, and he trying to get them to reveal the secrets of the spirits—until at midnight a bell sounded all over the house. The two women grew silent. The squat veiled lady appeared at the door of the kitchen. She beckoned him with a gloved hand.

At this point in the telling of the story, Houdini became agitated. He pushed aside his food, ran his hand through his thick, frizzy hair so that it stood on end. He hopped up from the settee and jumped onto his hands, walked around the hotel room on them, leapt back up. Finally, he faced the fireplace, his back to me. "I spent two hours with Mrs. Winchester, and then she returned my bathing costume, freshly laundered, and my milk can emptied and cleaned as well. She graciously ordered round her car to take me back to my hotel. Unfortunately, I had to walk through the lobby in my bathing costume carrying the milk can at dawn. But no one seemed to mind." He picked up an iron poker and fenced with it. "The end."

"The end?" I said.

"More or less." He continued to vigorously fence his invisible opponent.

"But. You haven't even described the house. What did you do with her for two long hours?" I shook the writing tablet that I'd been furiously taking notes in. "Finish the story, Sir. I implore you."

He dropped the poker and went back to standing on his hands. "I prefer not to."

"Please, Mr. Houdini. I need to know." I didn't add that I had a deadline to make.

He was still upside down. "If I tell you, you must swear not to write about it." He balanced on one arm and held his hand out for my notebook.

I had a decision to make, and fast, because I surmised if he stood up our conversation would be at an end. Here I must admit that I decided if the story were really good I would publish it anyway. I had a memory for details. He was balancing on both hands again, so I gently pressed the notebook between his teeth.

He righted himself, spit the little notebook into the fire, reseated himself on the settee, scraped up the last of the sour cream, cleared his throat, and continued. "The house. Labyrinthine. Outrageous. Offensive. Stairs ending at the ceiling. A stairwell leading to a door that opened onto a wall. An entire wing seemed to be blocked off." He said there must have been hundreds of rooms, all with the finest decorations, all eerily empty of inhabitants.

Strangest to him was the stairwell that Mrs. Winchester slowly led him up. It was narrow, wound round and round, the rise between each stair no more than an inch and a half, with a railing just a couple of feet off the stairs. Perfect for a miniature widow with joint pain.

At what seemed to be the very center of the house, Mrs. Winchester stopped in front of a pale green door. She gave him the once-over again, and then she knocked her cane against his shin, smartly, twice. Making sure he was solid most likely, he said, and not a spirit got up to look like Houdini. I laughed when he told me that, but he was not in a laughing mood. He'd thrown himself across his bed by this point, flung his arm over his golden eyes.

Mrs. Winchester nodded and turned, and he followed her in. She sat herself down in the small room that contained a table with two chairs, nothing more. The chairs were regular sized, and her feet did not touch the floor, but she had a small velvet-covered stool to rest them on. She unveiled herself.

She had a round, jowly face, a lot of grey hair piled on top of her head, a large bosom for one so small, and Houdini said, very small eyes. She had in front of her one of those children's novelties, a Ouija board.

Houdini sat down in the other chair.

"You may quietly observe," she said. "I have most important business to attend."

"May I inquire about the nature of this business, Madam?"

"I must consult the spirits about an addition to the house they lately specified."

"But why do they insist on this endless production?"

"I don't know."

"You don't know?"

"I know they like to see their plans come to fruition. I know it comforts them."

"But do you not long to be free of them? I am, forgoing modesty, the greatest escapologist in the world. Perhaps I can assist in your release."

"And then what should I do?"

Mr. Houdini was a bit at a loss, not being an expert in how rich old ladies spent their time. "Go to the theater?" he ventured. "Give money to charitable institutions? Paint tea cups?"

Mrs. Winchester rolled her eyes. "I must begin. It is a laborious process of communication, and I only have two hours."

"Madness," I remarked to Houdini. "Didn't you demand to know the point of all this useless construction?"

"How could I? When I have dedicated my life to locking myself up and freeing myself for people's amusement."

"Can you help me first?" Houdini asked Mrs. Winchester. "I want to speak to my dearest Mamala."

"Was she killed by a Winchester rifle?" Mrs. Winchester asked.

"She died of a stomach problem while I was abroad. I never got to say good-bye. But can't you ask your friends to rummage around for her?"

"They are not my friends," Mrs. Winchester said. But she asked out loud, "Can you locate Mr. Houdini's mother?" Then she sat patiently, her fingers lightly touching the planchette, which was wooden and shaped like a heart with a hole at its center. The planchette moved slowly over the board to the word YES.

"How is she?" Houdini asked eagerly. "Tell her I love her. Tell her I miss her."

"Slow down, slow down," Mrs. Winchester grumbled. She asked, "How is she?"

The planchette was still, then moved over the NO, then spelled out ENGLISH.

"What does that mean?" Houdini asked.

"They can't understand her. She's speaking in a foreign tongue."

"Hasn't any Jew ever been killed by a Winchester rifle? Tell them to tell her to speak English."

She said, "Tell her to speak English." Mrs. Winchester slowly spelled out: WHAT WITH THE SHMATE?

"Oh." Houdini looked down at the kimono. "A shmate is a rag."

"That's imported Japanese silk," Mrs. Winchester said. "I need to get to work. They only convene between midnight and two am. When I'm done, if there's time, you can speak to your impertinent mother again."

Mrs. Winchester asked architectural questions aloud, then the Ouija board spelled out the answers. She took notes on a grey tablet with a pencil. Sometimes she argued or asked the Ouija board to be more specific.

Houdini observed politely for thirty-seven minutes. Then he began to crack his neck and fingers, later his toes. Houdini amused himself by doing stretches and calisthenics. Push-ups, sit-ups. He practiced his handstands, then his handstands on one arm. He stretched his head between his legs. He managed a one-armed handstand on the chair.

The Widow Winchester was completely absorbed, not interested in the slightest that the great Harry Houdini was giving her a one-man show. For his part, he declared that watching the old woman work the Ouija board for an hour and fifteen minutes was the most boring performance he had ever witnessed.

Finally, he put his head down on the table. Did he fall asleep? He wasn't sure. He closed his eyes, and when he opened them the room was crowded with the dead. He was absolutely sure they were dead, right away, not because they were vaporous, which they were not, and not even because they floated a little off the ground, just enough so that you could slide a piece of paper underneath, which they did, and not because they moved about by exhaling a cold, dank breath that propelled them this way and that, according to the way they angled their chins, which they also did, but because they all had terrible gunshot wounds.

Half a face shattered to the bone, the back of the head blasted away, a burst of red on a waistcoat, an arm dangling, useless. They were not active wounds, there was no blood leakage, but they were forever unhealed and disconcerting nonetheless. It was loud in there, too, because they were all arguing with each other and with Mrs. Winchester about their joint building project.

And then pressed into a corner, Houdini spied a bony-faced old lady with a wisp of a grey topknot in a long white nightgown. It was his darling Mama

Weisz. Houdini shouldered his way through the busy, grisly group until he reached his little mama. They embraced, held hands, he wept, she stroked his face. By his calculation, factoring in his possible nap, they had approximately thirty-three minutes together.

She inquired about his health and about his wife Bess, but mostly she wanted to talk about food. She told him that was what she missed most—eating. They reminisced about shmaltz herring, kreplach, borscht, fried chicken hearts, pupicks. He grinned at me. "She had such a yen for Farmer's Chop Suey, it was infectious.

"How I miss her cooking," he said to me. "Which is funny, because she really wasn't a very good cook. Her matzo balls were rocks. Her chicken soup tasted like hot water that a chicken had maybe rested in for a minute or two before flying on to more important matters."

They whispered to each other, pressed close by the animated, arguing crowd. Mama Weisz said Houdini's breath smelled sweetly of orange zest with a fresh hint of celery. She said the breath of everyone where she was smelled like nothing, or like mud, and anyway breath was used exclusively for locomotion on the other side.

"But Mama, how is it? This afterlife? Is it paradise?"

"It could be worse," Mama Weisz replied, "but there's high unemployment, about 100 percent. That's why these shmucks are so excited."

"That was when she asked me to breathe on her face," Houdini said, his voice no longer sounding so British. "We held our hands together, and I breathed and she closed her eyelids and opened her mouth to take in my breath, and she said things like 'ah' and 'warm' and 'salty' and 'tart' and then the next thing I knew the bell rang, and I was standing in that corner by myself." Mr. Houdini lay on the bed, quiet and still.

"But what then?" I asked.

"Mrs. Winchester slid off her chair and unlocked the door of her séance room. The butler was standing there. 'Please show Mr. Houdini out,' she said." The last thing she said to Houdini was, "I will make sure my milk is inspected from now on."

"I was so overcome with my experience I said nothing," Houdini whispered. "I didn't thank her. I didn't ask to return."

I felt overcome myself. I sat down on the side of the bed. "But, Mr. Houdini, what do you think really happened? Do you think you were drugged? Do you think she mesmerized you in some manner?"

"I don't know," he said, "but it was the most important experience of my life."

To be honest, the narrative unnerved me. There was no way to uncover the truth. I didn't know what to do with it. I don't remember our leave-taking. That week I turned in a piece about the elaborate plans to ship the Liberty Bell back to Philadelphia after the Exposition. I never told the story, and for years I put it out of my mind.

The headline for the next forty years of my life could have been, "Heady Times These." I married late, we had a daughter, and my sister and mother lived with us, too. I never rode a motorbike cross-country, but in the twenties I investigated corruption in the San Francisco mayor's office and in railroad regulation. In the thirties I wrote about the kids who left Frisco to fight in the Spanish Civil War, in the forties I wrote about imprisoned conscientious objectors, and in the fifties about the thirty-two University of California professors fired for not signing anti-communist loyalty oaths.

My own mother died in '38, my sister in '65. My daughter's a single mom, lives in Sacramento with the grandchildren, Isaac and Sadie. When my wife passed away of the cancer in 1970, I retired here to West Palm Beach. Ten years I've been here now.

But you just got here, Buster, so I'll give you the rundown. This retirement home got the shuffleboard, we got B'nai B'rith. The big sport is playing bumper cars in our Lincoln Continentals to nab the spot closest to the entrance of the restaurant in time for the early bird special. I like watching *M*A*S*H*, and, believe it or not, I've started reading the Talmud. I still dance the Hustle sometimes alone in my room, and I send money to plant trees in Israel in the names of all my dead relatives. But mostly there's finally time to look back, turn it all over in my mind, cogitate so to speak.

For example, I wonder what Houdini would have thought about World War II, about the six million of our people who never escaped. Or what Mrs. Winchester would have thought about the millions killed by the M1 produced by the very same Winchester Corporation. Imagine how crowded that séance room would be now, how endless that mansion.

As far as I know, Houdini only returned to the Winchester Spirit House one more time, after Sarah Winchester died in her sleep. In 1924 Houdini got himself invited on a tour of the mansion at midnight, but nothing happened, at least that's what he told the newspapers. In the article he sounded bitter. Houdini himself died in 1926 of a burst appendix. His last request, so they say, was to order out for Farmer's Chop Suey.

That last request makes me wonder about my mother, and the mysteries of mothers in general. How did she conjure that endless love for me? What would it be like to be in that séance room, so the Widow Winchester could bring my mother to me, and my sister, and my darling wife, even if just for thirty-three minutes.

But so far I've had no ghostly visitations from my beloveds. Even Houdini and Mrs. Winchester have been quiet.

Still, what energy we had back then! What verve! Am I right, Buster? I thought we were so different, I searching for the truth, they trying to escape it, but the truth is we're all the same, me, Houdini, Mrs. Winchester—we believed! In breaking down walls or in building them, but we gave it everything we had. No holding back, no quitters allowed.

I worry about my grandchildren, Isaac and Sadie, two pale, little fatherless things all the way back in California. America in escape from itself, as they say, that's California. Where do you go from there? They call them the MTV generation, because they like that meshuganeh dancing on television, or they call them the latchkey generation. When their dad moved out I came for a while to help out. That schlemiel barged in one day, a fight erupted between him and my daughter, loud, a dish smashed.

When I finally got the bum to leave, I found Isaac and Sadie up in their bedroom. They'd made this higgledy-piggledy fort with stuffed animals and a chair. When I spoke to them, Isaac said, "We can't hear you or see you or nothing. This is a magic cave." Oy vey. For some reason, I thought of Hansel and Gretel lost in the forest, though they were right there in the bedroom. Hard to imagine them titans of the twentieth century, am I right?

Maybe that's not fair. They're sweet kids, Sadie and Isaac, I hope they'll be okay. I'm leaving them money, maybe it will help.

But it's still our century, am I right, Buster? The show's not over, am I right?

Quiero Bailar Slow with You Tonight

The first time we had sex, my lover whispered, "Sadie, I have never made love in English before."

I came as if everything were pouring out of me, and afterwards, with our foreheads touching, I sighed, "Que cosa mas linda." I don't speak Spanish.

"What did I just say?"

"It means the prettiest thing," he smiled.

I looked up at the ceiling as if I could see through it to the sky.

He slid his hand gently over my breast. "You are espactacular," he said, and I believed him.

When my lover was fourteen, in Santiago de Chile, he and his novia decided to make love. Both virgins, they searched for a place to perform the passionate operation. They rejected a park bench, an alley, then a bush, all of which were deemed too public or too dirty (this is characteristic of my lover, who is fastidious and also a gentleman). It grew late, the curfew horn blew, the yellow street lamps shone on empty sidewalks, but their passion overruled their sense.

I've never been to Santiago, but sometimes I picture it cool and foggy like summer mornings here on the Central Coast of California. Or, I imagine the young couple holding hands, wandering through billowing fog in an old black and white movie.

Finally, they climbed under a bridge. My lover had just pressed his lips to his novia's breast when a military police officer exposed them with his flashlight. This was during the dictatorship: people their age were both blowing up bridges and disappearing for doing nothing at all.

My lover stood in front of his novia in the harsh circle of light while she arranged her shirt. He told the armed officer that the girl had lost her bracelet over the bridge—they were looking for it. She held up her empty wrist for proof. The officer, who was also young, smirked and trained his flashlight on her misbuttoned blouse. They were all quiet while she re-buttoned, and the officer reached his decision, his gun still holstered.

At sunrise they found themselves dispiritedly jerking each other off on the park bench they had earlier rejected.

This novia wore a scent that drove my lover wild. He remembers it was by Avon, but not the name. He says that if I find this scent and wear it, he will marry me. He says this lightly, with a laugh. We never talk about the fact that his research fellowship, and thus his visa, runs out in three months.

My lover sends me torrid emails about the ferocity of his love: "Sadie," he writes, "I just wanted you to have a message when you open your email. Not just any message but one that could convey the exhilaration and happiness I felt yesterday. It is as if you were nuclear charged and your sexy particles were spreading all over around me. Do you think our love is like C14 and will last thousands of years, so that the beasts or whatever the hell is still living in the planet by then will know that one day, one morning, I felt your love and loved you?"

I send an email to Avon: "I have a very particular question for you. What fruity fragrance would have been popular around 1979 in Chile? You see, the man I am seeing cannot forget this scent that he once smelled on a girlfriend all those years ago. He says that if I can find that perfume, he will marry me. He doesn't remember the name, but he knows it was Avon. Any leads at all would be most helpful."

My lover wonders, what if on that night with his novia, the military police had not discovered him? What if he and his novia had successfully completed the unprotected act, what if she had gotten pregnant? He would have married at sixteen. He would now be living with five loud children and an exhausted wife in a crowded apartment in Santiago, working a government job, instead of studying on a one-year post-graduate fellowship here at the university in this pretty honky-tonk tourist town on the coast of California. He would never have met me.

I used the money my Grandpa Albert left me to open my own place, Bierce Park Books. I carry used books and videos. My Jewish immigrant grandfather was a journalist, plus he had a sense of humor, so I think he would have liked my store: two saggy green velvet armchairs, wooden shelves a friend built for me, an old cash register I found at the flea market, books stacked in the bathroom, the whole place smelling slightly of mold and dust. It's comfortable, and everything's arranged in my own way. Like, say you're searching for the old children's book, *The Secret Garden*. You'll find it in the section labeled, "Great Escapes and Hidden Hideaways" along with the 1993 film with Maggie Smith, the one with the beautiful time-lapse photography of the plants growing; *Miraculous Escapes*, a short story collection by local writer Dave Tanaka; the 30th anniversary edition DVD of *Alive*; *The Mysterious Disappearance of Ambrose Bierce;* an illustrated biography of Houdini; Edward Said's *Orientalism* and *My Secret Garden*, an anthology of women's sexual fantasies.

I've spent six days a week in my store for the past two years, wearing jeans or long skirts and sweaters, drinking tea, listening to world music, arranging and rearranging my things.

That's how we met. He came in while I was cataloguing. He said, "How ridiculous. So Gringolandia, so California. This is a search engine masquerading as a used book store." I'm used to new customers' irritation or confusion, but his voice sounded delighted, and I looked up.

I don't know why it happens this way. Why you can go years, and then one man wakes your heart up with a painful jolt. I can admit there are men who are more handsome, at least in the movies, but he appeared backlit. There was a precision and clarity to him—his smile, his long-lashed brown eyes, his thick, dark hair beginning to recede in the front. He made the rest of the world turn foggy and grey.

When I ask him about Chile, he leans back in his chair, crosses his ankles, and says, "You would love the food, mi reina."

You can buy empanadas right off the street on the way to classes at the university, little golden turnovers filled with savory meat, egg, olives, and raisins. Or buy Italianos outside the National Library, hot dogs with mayonnaise, tomato, and mashed avocado. At home, the angelic, hardworking mother will make soup with squash, spaghetti and meat, and rosquitas, sweet little donuts flavored with lemon or orange. She will keep them warm until you return after a long day of studying. Next day she'll wake at five a.m. to make breakfast while you begin to read. Soft boiled eggs and pieces of bread mixed with oil and salt in a cup. Strong tea with lots of sugar.

He calls his mother every Sunday and asks first, "Mami, what are you cooking today?"

He's studying U.S. fusion cuisine, who eats it, who cooks it, and why. He spends a lot of time in back kitchens with his tape recorder, talking to Mexican workers. I help with his research. We go to Japanese restaurants and order cream cheese and lox sushi. We go to Mexican restaurants and eat organic Thai burritos. He shakes his head, laughs, and writes pages of notes in his little book. My brother Isaac's wife Diane is the chef/owner of a 'California Umami' restaurant. I take him there, we sit at a candlelit table, and he says, "These people carry their homeland on their backs. They cook in the Third World and the food magically appears in the First."

I say, "What about Diane? She cooks back there."

He says, "Of course, the head chef is white, but after that it's white waiters in the front, Latino kitchen help in the back. Forget the Rio Grande. That's the true border, right there, the door between the kitchen and the dining room."

His own apartment is not a fusion of anything. It's pure Costco. He has huge boxes of cereal and tubs of margarine and his freezer is filled with frozen dinners. The only furniture is a cot and a foosball table he bought at Costco. We play all the time. He always wins, and then he flashes his triumphant smile, a wall of perfectly white teeth, but I don't give up.

The third Avon representative I have been forwarded to writes back, "It's not surprising that your Señor recalls a sweet perfume in 1979 in Chile, because if I remember my history, 1979 stunk in Chile. White Shoulders, Whisper, and My Lady were the best-selling Avon scents in 1979, but I don't know if we exported them to Chile. I'll forward your email to someone who might."

"Did 1979 stink in Chile?" I ask my lover. "And do these names mean anything to you: White Shoulders, Whisper, My Lady?"

"Yes," he says, "it stunk like death, and no, the names mean nothing to me." He has two months left on his visa.

He's teaching me Spanish. He writes the words on yellow Post-its from the giant batch he bought at Costco. We tape them all over my house. On the cup, taza, on the bed, cama, the door—puerta. The television, televisión.

He holds me with his eyes, says each word slowly, as if it were a magic incantation that will coax a golden coin from my mouth. He looks so hopeful and watches my mouth so intently it makes me laugh instead of speak Spanish.

He bounces on his toes, laughs too, but says, "Please, mi gringuita, try."

"Puerta," I say, the middle of the word twisting awkwardly in my mouth.

He's bouncing again. "Excellent! Perfecto! That's it! That's it!"

I say, "You know very well that's not perfecto. You're so goddamn cheerful and bouncy. You remind me of Tigger in *Winnie the Pooh*. Did you ever read *Winnie the Pooh*?"

"Of course. You'd be Piglet."

"I'm not a pink little wimp."

"Oh, yes, you are."

I write Bouncy Bouncy Bouncy on a Post-It and smack it on his butt.

He writes Cerdito, Little Pig, and posts it on my forehead.

I post Winnie The Poop on his shoulder.

He posts The Honey Pot between my legs.

We look at each other, smiling.

"Now you'll see," he says.

"So will you."

We both begin writing on Post-Its.

Then we hold our message hidden in our hands and face each other. "Let me see what you wrote," he says.

"You first."

He presses his gently onto my chest. It says, Te amo in his upright writing.

I stick mine on his chest, which says I love you.

When we kiss the sound of two small pieces of paper brushing against each other comes up from our hearts.

I cc everyone at Avon who has passed me on: "I'm not sure if you realize the gravity of the situation. If I do not discover the name of the fruity fragrance popular around 1979 in Chile I may lose my lover forever. Please help. This is not a joke."

We are walking downtown at night, holding hands, past a clown singing, "You are the Sunshine of My Life," past a man sliding enormous bubbles out of a silver hoop, past gaggles of young boys with sagging shorts and skateboards, past dreadlocked white girls in ripped hemp, while lowriders parade past us.

He says, "Maybe you just love me because I'm Latin-American. I'm your Zorro, your Don Juan. My brutal English turns you on."

"Do you love me because I'm Jewish?" I answer back, quick. But I look at his face and he's holding his mouth in a soft, damaged way, like a listing life raft, and I try to really think about the question. I say, "I love you because you love things. You love books, you love food, you love women, you love me. Things surprise you, they delight you. So many men I know don't love anything. We're the whatever generation."

"I'm not a whatever kind of man," he says, and kisses me right there on the street in a not-whatever way.

We're eating dinner at my house, take-out from a Pan-Asian restaurant, and he tells me he read that a British academic journal decided to boycott Israel, and then fired two American Jews on its board in order to honor the boycott. He shakes his head, says, "Absurd," and laughs. He seems, as usual, delighted.

My face gets hot, and I say, "Sometimes I think the left is as anti-Semitic as the right."

"That's crazy," he laughs. He covers my big hand with his small hand. They are almost exactly the same size, except his is tan with dark hair and mine is pink and hairless. "The left stands for freedom and human rights. There are so many Jews on the left."

I take my hand away and dig my fork around in my bowl. "How many Jews have you even met in your entire life?"

He tells me about this Chilean-Jewish scientist he was introduced to at a party at the university who supports a Palestinian state.

"How is that even relevant?" I ask. "From what I've heard there are a lot more Nazis than Jews in Chile anyway."

His fork is arrested in midair, dangling noodles. He says, "It's not the Nazis that nearly destroyed my country, it's the United States. The U.S. is supporting the Israeli fascist regime just like they supported Pinochet in my country and apartheid in South Africa."

"Yes, Israel needs a two-state solution, but Ariel Sharon is not Pinochet. You don't understand Jewish history."

"This is a ridiculous conversation. You're not even really Jewish, you don't even go to Jewish church."

"Over a hundred years ago, my Grandpa Albert's grandfather sat him on his knee and told him, 'Never forget you are a Jew.' Then Grandpa Albert left Warsaw with his mother and sister. His grandfather died of starvation in the Warsaw ghetto." I'm almost crying. "We gave you Freud, Marx, Einstein, Emma Goldman, we even gave you God. We've given everything we have, and it's still not enough. You just turn your backs on us and walk away."

"What are we talking about here?" he says.

"I don't know. Everything."

"Everything is more than enough," he says, and touches my cheek.

Finally, an Avon representative emails me. There were three scents put out in the 1970's that were exported to Chile:

1. Sweet Honesty, 1973
"Floral fragrance of rose, hyacinth, musk, amber, and spices"

2. Timeless, 1974
"Subtle spices and florals with ambery undertones, warm moss and wood notes; nuances of incense enhance its long-lasting qualities"

3. Candid, 1977
"Long-lasting creation of Jasmine, tuberose and ylang-ylang is underscored by the warm nuances of sandalwood oakmoss and vetiver"

I hope this helps!" are the last words from Avon.

I forward the Avon email to him and he responds quickly: "I am sure it was Sweet Honesty! Or at least that's what I want to believe, more than anything. I love you sweetly and honestly."

I close the store early and go home to make a celebratory dinner. I cook empanadas and matzah ball soup. It takes me the rest of the day. When he comes over he brings me a new CD, an anthology of love songs from around the world. My empanadas are a little thick-skinned, but he says they're muy rica for a first try. He has three bowls of soup and says he loves my "hard, little balls." The wine is Chilean and reminds me of blackberries. A Hawaiian love song comes on and we both get up and begin to hula. He moves his arms in two little waves and frisks his hips. The next track begins, and it is a gravelly male voice moaning, "Quiero Bailar Slow with You Tonight," fingers aching over a steel string guitar. I run to my bedroom and come back.

I turn over my wrists to him and he lifts each one, presses his nose to it, and breathes deeply. Then he pushes my hips against the kitchen counter and breathes into my neck. "Yes, this is it, this is it. I want to dance slow with you tonight." His hips hula hard and slow against mine. "And I will talk to my department about extending my research fellowship."

A few days later, four to be exact, he calls me from his office, right when I'm about to leave for the store, and tells me that he needs to talk to me. He'll come by around noon. His voice sounds echoey and weird. I think, Do not be paranoid. Then I think, I am not going to let him screw this up.

I pull on my new thigh-high black boots that he hasn't seen yet, then a short skirt. I do that elegant thing

31

where you spritz the air with perfume and walk through it, but then I get nervous that it's too subtle and squeeze the Sweet Honesty on my neck, hair and wrists, too.

When I get to the store, I play my new world love sampler CD, loudish. All morning, while I'm going over my inventory, fragments of arguments sift through my head: But you promised. I found the perfume. You said you loved me. You have a major mother complex you need to escape. Or simply, Don't leave me.

Mr. Nowicki, an old man they call the Mayor of Bierce Park, comes in. He shows up every few weeks to complain about the store, never buys anything, but this time he asks for *Miraculous Escapes* by Dave Tanaka. I show him where it is, invite him to peruse the whole section.

Ridiculous, he says, but then, miraculously, he peruses. I pull out the big picture book on Houdini to show him. I tell him my Grandpa Albert interviewed Houdini back in the day.

"This is a children's book," he says. "You can't mix kids' books in with grown-up books, that will attract perverts."

My thinking goes something like—children's books, children, babies, a baby. A baby.

I know it's a desperate thought, and I try to disown it. But it's such a solid, old-fashioned argument, one Mr. Nowicki himself might approve. And my lover is a gentleman, so I know he'd recognize its worth.

Then the little bell on the door tinkles. I say excuse me to Mr. Nowicki and turn and there he is. As soon as I look at the damaged way he's holding his mouth I know I was right to be prepared.

The first thing he says is, "Where did you get those boots? They remind me of the military." He walks behind the counter and lets himself fall onto a wooden chair, and before I can begin my defense—of my boots, of our relationship, of the United States—he says, "I cannot leave my country. I can't do it." He begins to cry quietly. He sits there sagging, his glasses dirty. "This place is a wonderful carnival, but it is not my home."

"Don't say that." My mind's all jumbled up. I don't know what to say first.

"There were these Australian photographers," he says, "traveling all around the world. In each place they would put a notice in the paper: 'Come at 8AM to have a group portrait of your country taken, naked.' More people came out in Chile than any other country. My whole family went, and all our friends, almost our whole neighborhood. It was a cold day, winter, drizzling, and there we were, rubbing our hands together, making jokes. Right at 8AM we all undressed, our jeans and suits and dresses lying at our feet, thousands of us, all together for the world to see. Laughing and freezing desnudos." He looks at me. "I cannot forget that." His voice turns into a mumble then, but I think I hear him say, Mi Mama, and then the Andes, which I have never heard him mention before, and finally, incomprehensibly, the subway system in Santiago and the proliferation of cheap, natural juices.

I hear myself say, "I'll go with you. To Santiago." The city tastes acidic in my mouth.

"What about your store? You would lose everything."

I literally get down on my knees, then, my stiff new black boots cutting into my legs, and put my clasped hands in his lap. "I have something to tell you."

He takes notice. "What?"

I think a lot of things, quickly, as you can imagine: crowded apartments, crowds of people, I wonder if there were pregnant naked women in the Chilean photograph. But mostly I think of his novia, how her memory still smells sweet because of what didn't happen.

I look up from my position on the floor and Mr. Nowicki is standing on the other side of the counter. "How much are these books? They don't even have prices on them."

"You can have them," I say.

He looks surprised.

"Go ahead, it's fine, take them."

"No way to run a business," he says. We both watch him limp out the door.

I get up off the floor and sit in the chair.

"What did you want to say?" he asks.

I realize my store reeks of cheap perfume. I answer, "Nothing. Just that you are so old-fashioned. Don't you know that borders have no meaning anymore? What about *Tarzan*, the Disney version? Jane stays in the jungle."

Surprisingly, he shoots back that in *Pocahontas*, the Disney version, Pocahontas remains with her people.

"Aha!" I say, gaining a little ground, "but in real life she married and had a baby and travelled to England."

"And died there, homesick and alone." He smiles sadly. "That's the real story."

At the airport, I wave and he waves, all through the security check. They stop him for a pat down and I can see him roll his brown eyes. I have a sudden wild hope that they will return him to me. Then it's over, they hurry him on. He turns and mouths, "Sadie, I love you."

Two hours later he calls me from Texas, the layover. We talk until they call last boarding for his plane. He has to hang up in a hurry. He says, "We will be together, again. I'll call you from home." He sounds honest, and sweet. I sit in my sagging green velvet chair, alone in my closed store, and cry. It sounds loud and ugly. I think bitterly, This is the real world music.

But I don't believe that, or at least, I don't believe only that. In fact, my favorite Spanish word is Ojalá. It has such a breathy, warm, open sound. It has Arabic roots, from pre-1492 Spain where once upon a time Jews and Arabs and Latinos all lived together, surrounded by arches and mosaic tiles, by the smell of rose, hyacinth, musk, and amber. Oh Allah, it comes from, Oh Allah, I entreat you. It means hope.

We Are
The Same
People

"Jeez, Diane," my husband Isaac says, "someone's messed with your getaway car."

It looks like maybe a third-grade girl or a fairy has gotten hold of it. The station wagon's been painted neon pink and covered from fender to roof in plastic butterflies. The algae-scented wind blows up off the lake—the live oak branches around our summerhouse wave, the hundreds of tiny plastic wings shiver.

I circle the station wagon, growling, fists clenched, ready to destroy this My Little Pony Paradise, but then I look over at my daughter Lilah. She's still caged in our SUV, arms raised, palms up in adulation. Speechless with desire.

And then my husband Isaac shakes his head and says, "Diane, you know this is your brother's idea of a practical joke."

My fists unclench, I roll my eyes and unseatbelt Lilah; she scrambles out, runs her fingers gently over the plastic wings.

Leaving Lilah to worship in peace, Isaac and I each take a bag and head down the few yards to the cottage, Isaac groaning that it must be over a hundred degrees.

I'm trying not to let the defacement of the getaway car ruin everything. There are really only two places in the world where my heart isn't full of twigs—my restaurant kitchen and here. Here's just my family's old fishing camp which my brother Dave and I now own together, peeling white paint and red trim, kitchen/ living room with a smoky fireplace and a sleeping porch, a bedroom and bathroom on the floor below, no neighbors on the long gravel drive. Every year we half-heartedly prune the overgrown rose bush and lilacs and tie down the sagging grape vine and scrub the slime off the stairs down to the water and cut back the blackberry prickers and trap the mice and kill the spiders. It's on the edge of the biggest natural lake in California. It's called Clear Lake, though it grows a thick coat of green every summer, which keeps the tourists away. And it's like the inside of a convection oven most days in September. Isaac hates the heat, but I am often cold where we live on the coast. Clear Lake is the place I finally warm up down to my bones. Isaac won't let Lilah swim in the possibly harmful blue-green algae, has bought her a kiddie pool instead, but my brother Dave and I still go in, emerging like toxic creatures from the green lagoon.

I pull open the ripped screen. Isaac turns on a fan in the living room and plucks at the bottom of his t-shirt to air out. Dave isn't upstairs, and it looks like he's cleared out of the downstairs bedroom. I drop the suitcase on the chenille bedspread.

I'm on my knees unzipping our bags when Lilah sneaks up behind me, grabs my hair, pulls back my head, and plants a kiss on my lips. This kiss is so hard I can feel her teeth on my teeth. This kiss knocks me backwards. She stands over me, grabs my hands and says, "Let's dance. We're in love."

I say, "Why don't you explore?"

She gets down on her hands and knees and crawls under the bed.

I say, "There's spiders under there."

"There's a toy."

"Okay," I say, throwing Isaac's shirts into one drawer, his rolled underwear and tube socks into the little one above. I turn for my pile, and there's Lilah, sitting on the rag rug. She wags a pink dildo at me, "Hi. My name is Na Na." The dildo is shaped like a beaver. Lilah hits a switch and the tongue on the beaver begins to vibrate. "Can I keep her?" Lilah asks.

"That's a grown-up toy," I say.

"I'll be careful."

"It's Dave's private toy, okay, honey?"

"I want it."

"Lilah, I'm sorry, it's not yours." I reach for it.

She hugs the beaver to her chest. "Unfair!"

Lilah begins to sob, and I have to call Isaac in. He holds her while I wrench the dildo out of her hand. "Dave," Isaac sighs. He carries Lilah outside, whispering soothingly in her ear.

I let the beaver tongue my palm for a bit, then shut it down. I get a paper bag, drop the dildo in, write Dave's stage name "Dove" on it in purple crayon and put it on the kitchen counter. I leave the house in search of my brother.

Beside the house, Lilah and Isaac are crouched, studying a lizard doing push-ups.

I look up then, and what do we have here, a tree house under construction in the many-armed oak tree twenty yards from the house. Dave, and what must certainly be his new girlfriend, grinning down at us. Except for tool belts, both of them are naked.

The general impression is as follows: Dave, 6'2", a red-brown color, extremely buff, his long equipment swaying nonchalantly. Beside him, the girlfriend, gold and pink, blue eyes, blond eyelashes, white-blond hair tied with a leather thong, nose peeling. She's got blond hair on her legs, but she's shaved her kooch back to its newborn state.

They look straight out of that *Blue Lagoon* movie, as schmaltzy as the car. "Really?" I grimace.

I look over at Isaac, his face raised in goddess worship. I roll my eyes, walk closer to the tree house.

"This is Anna," Dave says.

"You're the one that did that to the getaway car, aren't you?" I say.

"Just some paint, a glue gun and a trip to the Dollar Store," she says modestly.

"I gave it to her," Dave says.

"You gave it to me," I say.

"I'm so sorry if there was a misunderstanding," the girlfriend says, flushing.

"You haven't driven it in years, Diane."

"Not the point."

"Why is it called getaway?" Lilah asks.

"Good question," Isaac says.

"Yeah, Diane, why do you call it the getaway car?" Dave grins.

I laugh, teeth bared, pretend to let it go. "So, how are you guys doing?" I say. "Be honest."

Dave smirks. "Hanging in there."

The girlfriend glances at him with a worried smile.

Isaac's still crouched in the scrub, staring up.

By now, Lilah has rushed over. She pulls her shirt off and begs to climb up.

"You'll get splinters," Isaac calls. He's finally regained his power of speech. "It's not a tree house for kids."

I lift her, Dave reaches down and pulls her up by the arms.

"Steady!" Isaac says.

The girlfriend keeps a gentle hand on Lilah's bare back, while Lilah leans over the railing. She has this big, goopy smile on her face, but then Lilah reaches in her pants pocket and lets fall a bouquet of plastic wings.

The girlfriend's smile wilts.

"Lilah!" I say, pretending horror. "What did you do?"

The girlfriend pulls Dave's faded, ripped T-shirt over her tool belt and swings down the ladder like a trapeze artist. Then she and Isaac busy themselves picking up all the little plastic bits amongst the ferns.

"The bet is still on," I stage whisper up at Dave. "And if I win, I want the car back, too." Dave just grins at me as he passes Lilah down.

Dave is a screenwriter in LA. On the phone this past June he tells me he has fallen for an artist/musician. "Anna plays the electric violin with an all-girl band! It's a performance art thing! They use her sculpture as a backdrop!"

"A little bit country, a little bit rock 'n' roll." This is sotto voce, so Lilah won't wake from her nap. The moment she wakes, even before she opens her eyes, she will begin to moan, 'Mommy, I need you.' "What's her sculpture like?"

"I haven't seen them. It might be a turnoff."

"What's her band called?" Still whispering.

"Clitorama!" We both snicker. "She made me a ceramic butterfly pin!" We're laughing now. "Stop it, Diane, don't screw with romance."

"Helga isn't going to last the summer," I whisper. "Three months is your record."

"It's Anna. Want to make a bet?"

"I bet you don't make it through Labor Day weekend."

"What do I get if I win?" he says.

"You get Helga. What do I get if I win?" I ask.

"You leave Isaac and move in with me. You are, after all, my longest lasting relationship."

There's this little sizzle in my chest. "Are you serious?" I say.

Dave says, "Labor Day or bust!"

While Dave and Helga get dressed, I choose *Alive!*, one of my childhood favorites, from the bookshelf and lay myself out on the hammock on the porch. Lilah climbs in after me with a clutch of naked Barbies, begins to whisper to herself. The Barbies, named Mommy and Lilah, are planning their nuptials.

Dave and Helga appear. Dave in cargo pants, a green t-shirt, and work boots, Helga in a little blue thrift store sundress with a daisy print. Cute. No bra. Dave says they are going to drive over to the bakery in Lucerne to get cinnamon raisin bread. This is a ritual of ours. Lilah asks if she can come, but Dave says he's going on his motorcycle, so before Lilah pitches a fit, Isaac retrieves Lilah from the hammock, says he'll take her out in the rowboat.

Helga and Dave keep bumping up against each other and giggling.

"Isaac! Put her life jacket on," I call irritably, although there is no way he would ever forget.

Dave followed me to UCSC, a year behind. This was the early nineties—it was all about androgyny for us, Bowie, Prince, and ever since we were kids, Michael Jackson. Before we'd go dancing we'd get dressed in my dorm room, put on our platform sneakers, our leopard-print coats, paint our nails metallic blue, middle-part our bowl cuts.

We called ourselves The Untouchables. If anyone asked one of us to dance we'd start doing our *Thriller* zombie routine, jerk our head to one side, kick out a leg, scare them away. It was better than drugs.

I was studying English but spending most of my time working at Oswald's, the best restaurant in town. Dave was majoring in economics. Then, no warning, he left. He moved to LA, waited tables, tried to act, then went to film school; and just when my father was despairing that Dave would always be a hobo, he changed his name to Dove and began to make a lot of money writing screenplays that never got produced.

Isaac was one of the chubby, doe-eyed guys in our dorm who had a crush on me. Everyone said he was a nice guy.

At our wedding reception, paid for by an inheritance from Isaac's Grandfather Albert, Dave and I sat on the back stone wall, watching Isaac dance with his nerdly little sister Sadie. Dave and I were sharing a cigar.

Dave said, "If you want, we can still run. I've got

the station wagon in the parking lot."

But I was feeling contented, Champagne and nicotine in my veins. I said, "I know you don't like Isaac."

"Untrue," Dave said. "I wouldn't care if I never saw him again, but at least we can rest assured he will do no harm."

"Exactly," I said. "Isaac is life insurance against the danger I pose to myself and others."

"I've got some extra insurance for you," Dave said. "I'm giving you the station wagon. Wedding present. I'll park it at Clear Lake. It'll be your getaway car."

A year later we had Lilah.

Isaac carries Lilah in from the boat, already asleep, her face hot and red, her hair plastered to her sweaty forehead. As he takes her down the stairs, still in her life preserver, she moans, "Mommy." I flinch, but she sleeps on. In *Alive!,* most of the soccer players are a couple of chocolate bars away from cannibalism. A discerning few will choose to die rather than take a bite of flesh. I hear the front door slam and Dave comes out to the porch. "Hi," he says, squashing his big self into the hammock, making it swing wildly. "She wants me to move in with her. We were in the tree house just now, and I told her I would need a lot of space. And she said she understood. It seems like we're getting somewhere." He winks.

"You know I hate winks. And get your legs off me."

He winks again, one eye, then the other. "She looks like Jessica Simpson, doesn't she?"

"Yeah, but not *Dukes of Hazzard* Jessica, more like fat Jessica," I say.

"Rude." We're both giggling now.

"Shh," I say. "You'll wake Lilah."

"Speaking of fat, I think you've been hitting the laxatives too hard, Di. You still look like a thirteen-year-old boy with a tit problem. A very small tit problem. If you move to LA, you'll have to insert a couple of plastic baggies in there. And you've got the same rat hair growing out of your chin from ten years ago. Ever heard of waxing, electrolysis, tweezers?"

"Yank it," I say.

Then we hear Helga yodeling, "Dove?"

"In here," Dave calls. Another wink, I pinch him, he yelps, and then Helga bounces in and actually climbs onto the hammock, causing it to sag to the floor. Her legs are all tangled up with mine. I try to wrench free. "It can't take the weight," I say, but they ignore me. "Doesn't the heat bother you?" I ask her.

"I like it," she says.

"Diane can't stand the cold," Dave says. "She'd never have survived in *Alive*. Plus, she chooses not to sweat, it's truly freakish."

"I think it's great that you're so close," Helga says.

"We're not that close. I'm just the only one who remembers his real name."

"So, Diane, Dove tells me you're a chef. What kind of food do you cook?"

"The good kind." Every time she moves, you get a glimpse of her Barbie doll breasts through the big armholes in her sleeveless daisy dress. Both of their legs are so sweaty they're sliming all over me. And she's got this musk on, of course.

"I love *The Moosewood Cookbook*. Do you ever cook from that?"

"Only if I want to pass out from boredom."

"What a bitch," Dave says.

"Dove!" Helga chirps.

Which wakes Lilah up—"Mommy, I need you!"—which puts an end to our getting-to-know-you talk.

I'm prepping dinner—making the marinade for the steak and the lime vinaigrette for the deep-fried Brussel sprouts. Helga and Dave decide to go swimming.

I say, "Take Lilah," so they do. I stand in the picture window facing the lake, drinking my horseradish-infused vodka. Dave and Helga strip naked again. Lilah watches them swim out, her back bowed, ankle-deep in her kiddie pool.

Isaac comes over. "Look at this," he says. He's holding the raisin bread loaf. The sweet cinnamon road that wound through the bread has been eaten away. "Lilah loves this bread," Isaac says. "Diane, look at this." He shows me the other two loaves, both hollow. "Do you really think your brother is responsible enough to be Lilah's godfather? You have to admit Sadie would be a better choice."

"Let's not get into this again."

"Remember what he said, when we asked him to be Lilah's guardian, he said, 'If you decide to die, give me six-month's notice, so I can change my life.'"

"He was joking."

"Look at them, they just left Lilah there in her pool. She could drown."

"Why don't you make her wear a life preserver in the kiddie pool? Maybe she should wear a life preserver 24/7, just in case."

"He doesn't pay any attention to her. It's an inappropriate choice."

"Dave is the person most like me in the world."

"You're not that much alike."

"The two of us together could potentially equal one competent parent."

Isaac's face spasms. "What are you talking about?"

"I need to start the grill," I say to Isaac, and leave to hunt up the charcoal.

At dinner, I try to join in on the conversation but Lilah has developed this strategy—whenever I turn away to talk, she cups my chin in her hand and pulls it back to her, so I give up and try to listen to Dave, Helga and Isaac over Lilah's conversation, which is about a purple stove she wants to buy me.

They're getting all chummy and slugging this aggressive Cab Helga bought and cutting big pieces of steak and eating with gusto. Helga glances at me. I've noticed she is always trying to make some kind of meaningful contact or figure me out or whatever. I stare back like a zombie until she can't take it anymore. She zeros in on Isaac instead, "So, what's your love story?"

Isaac smiles, "Oh gosh."

"Was it love at first sight?"

"I just liked her. Right away."

"He liked me because I was mean. I was always shocking him. I corrupted—"

"—Mommy, don't talk."

"I just want to tell—"

Lilah pulls my chin around to her.

Isaac says, "It's true, she doesn't ice things over.

But I fell in love with her on a day I saw her in the dorm kitchen. She didn't even have a meal plan. She was plating this perfect dinner for one, like one pork chop, three roasted carrots, a beet salad from one beet. I always seemed to attract women with eating disorders, you know the kind that chooses a chocolate cake, takes a few bites, then pours salt over it so they won't be tempted. Diane wasn't like that. She—"

"—Isaac's the kind of guy that attracts weirdos," Dave interrupts with his mouth full.

"Thanks, Dave," Isaac and I both say together.

"He always ends up pushing a homeless guy's wheelchair or taking the keys away from a drunk. He's God's designated driver," Dave says.

Helga says, "What I liked about Dove, immediately, was his openness. He's more like a woman that way."

"Why do women always think Dave is so feminine?" Isaac says. "I don't get it."

"Because he's sensitive," Helga says.

"Because while Dave's buying toilet paper," I say, "he's also making an advertisement about this hot guy named Dove who can't decide between Scott's and Ultra Soft. He does that subject/object thing that women do."

"You mean he's his own sex object," Isaac says.

"I'm your sex object, right Isaac?" Dave says.

"Heads up," I say to Dave, it's a game we play, I ping a Brussel sprout at him, he catches it in his mouth, chews, opens up and shows me the contents. We grin at each other.

"My mommy, not your mommy," Lilah says to Dave, pulling my chin toward her.

Helga changes the subject, asks Isaac about his

work as Director of Manpower, then they start talking about Helga's art.

I interrupt, "You must have some images of your work. Why don't you give us a show?"

She seems pleased and agrees.

I grin at Dave over their heads.

He mouths, "Cheater."

After dinner, I get Lilah into her pajamas, then we all squish onto the spineless couch with the laptop on the coffee table. Helga seems bashful and happy. We turn the lights off. Helga blocks the screen, fiddles with the settings. Lilah wants to click buttons, but Helga won't let her. Lilah's about to throw a fit, she's getting tired, but then Helga moves aside to reveal the first image, full screen.

We all stare at the veiny pink and red ceramic butterfly. It's spewing water from its lower thorax.

"That's good," Lilah says.

We laugh.

Helga clicks and there's another pink and red butterfly with water pouring out of it.

Isaac says in his usual respectful, interested way, "Whom do you see as your influences?"

I look over at Dave, his face half in shadow, half in light, grimacing like he's watching a horror movie.

Helga's ready to talk though. "Georgia O'Keeffe is a point of departure. I feel that representing the vagina as a butterfly, something that moves, rather than the static image of the flower is," she searches for the word in the air with her hands—"kinetic."

"So, the butterfly is pissing?" I say.

"Actually, the water represents female ejaculation."

"What?"

"You guys know that women can ejaculate. I mean, there's a documentary film about it."

"What are they ejaculating?" I ask.

Lilah isn't paying any attention to us. She presses her finger against the screen, trying to touch a wing.

"My butterflies ejaculate tap water."

"No, but—"

"—Let's look at some more," Dave interjects.

"Helga, can you do that?" I ask.

"Anna." Her face prunes up like I've finally insulted her.

"Sorry. Anna."

"Diane—" Dave says.

"Yes, I can," Helga says, all dignified.

"Yikes," I say, triumphantly.

When the show's over, Isaac, Lilah and I leave the happy couple to discuss art in private.

Isaac brushes Lilah's teeth while I stand in the doorway.

"Those butterflies sort of T-U-R-N-E-D   M-E O-N," he spells, while he earnestly scrubs Lilah's molars.

So many things go through my head, like, how much could we get for the house? Would it be enough for Dave and I to buy something in Silver Lake? The food scene in LA is incredible, but what about Lilah? I'd have to hire someone, a nanny, and Dave would help out, wouldn't he?

Then I realize Isaac is reading something in my face.

He says, "What."

"Nothing."

"What's wrong?"

"We can talk later."

"About what? Just give me the general subject."

"Tell us, Mommy."

They're both watching me way more attentively than I need or want. I open my mouth and what comes out is, "Passion."

"Passion?" Isaac and Lilah say together.

"What's passion, Mommy?" Lilah says.

"Passion is strong feelings, like excitement."

"So, now you want excitement? I thought you wanted security," Isaac says.

"I want passion," Lilah says.

Isaac throws the toothbrush into the sink. He walks into the bedroom, then back into the bathroom, then makes the round again. He's got his thinking cap on. Lilah and I watch him.

Isaac rubs his hands together. "Girls, I've thought of something exciting."

Lilah says, "Okay."

"Can we just put Lilah to bed?" I say.

"Diane, I can do excitement." Isaac grabs the flashlight and tells us to follow him out into the dark. "Let's go." He leads us out the back door and around the house. I can hear Dave and Helga murmuring to each other. It's chilly. We walk up the driveway, and he opens the door to the butterflied getaway car.

"What are you doing?" I say.

"We're going for a joyride."

"The key's hidden in the house," I say.

Isaac gestures towards the key, now adorned with a pink pom-pom, in the ignition. We put Lilah between us, she's bouncing up and down. She presses the button on the glove compartment and it pops open. She pulls out a Tootsie Pop, chocolate. "Can I have it?" I unwrap it for her.

Isaac whispers, "They'll hear the engine. We'll just roll out of the driveway." Isaac pulls the lights. Nothing. "When's the last time you started the car?" Isaac asks.

"A while ago," I say.

He hands me the flashlight and I open the door and shine it behind us. Isaac shifts the car into neutral. We hear the quiet crunch of gravel as we glide backwards down the incline of our driveway. He tries to turn the wheel to the left, to swing the car towards the road. "Steering wheel's locked."

I hear the squeak as Isaac pumps the breaks. "Breaks don't work," he says. He turns the key, but the car does not turn over. He tries the emergency break. Nothing.

We are backing rapidly towards the lake, gaining speed. I'm still hanging out the door, training the flashlight into the darkness. We go over a dip, and I bounce out of the car.

I hear Lilah scream, "Mommy." My shoulder hits a rock. The station wagon backs relatively smoothly over the dry grass, the open door flapping slightly. I am still holding the flashlight. I know Isaac and Lilah must be watching me, but the front windshield is black, and I can't see them. I stand up.

The car is now just a few yards from the water. The driver side door opens. Isaac, with Lilah in his arms, leaps. The getaway car bumps down the five log steps, both doors flapping, and slides, butt first, into the green water. It clunks suddenly to a stop, the algae closes over it up to the windows, the wings on the roof glint in the moonlight.

I stumble over to where Isaac crouches, gripping Lilah.

"Are you okay?" I ask.

Isaac is feeling Lilah's limbs. "We're okay," he says.

"You drowned my car," I say.

"That was Anna's art," Lilah says, staring at the sunken car. "We're in big trouble."

"That's true." I laugh angrily. "This will clinch it, definitely."

"You're in shock," Isaac says.

"We have to tell Dave."

"Wait—" Isaac says. "Let's just gather ourselves—"

But I'm heading for the house.

I squint in the light, Isaac and Lilah hiding behind me. Dave and Helga are sitting on the couch in what I immediately see is the breakup position. Each with their arms crossed, about two feet from each other, looking ahead. I am the icing on the cake.

"I thought you guys were asleep," Dave says.

"There's a slight problem with the butterfly mobile," I say.

"What?" Helga sits up and takes notice.

"The engine wouldn't turn over, so," Isaac begins.

"It's going to the Creativity Museum in San Francisco," Helga explains.

I pull some grass out of my hair. "I don't think so."

Helga jumps up, ready to save her baby. "What do you mean, what happened?"

"It fell in the lake," I say.

"It's the centerpiece of my show at the museum."

Isaac is literally hanging his head in shame. "I'm

52

so sorry, Anna. I take full responsibility. It was my idea. But, tomorrow, we can—"

Helga rushes out the door.

"Anna, wait—" Dave says.

I grin at Dave, give him the V for victory sign.

He says, "Lilah could have been killed."

I grin, but then I see he's not joking. He's looking at Lilah. We all three look at her, the lollipop stuck in her hair, covered in dirt, like some child who has already been killed.

I curl my V for Victory into a fist. I say, "Dave, that's something I wanted to talk to you about. Isaac and I have decided to put his sister Sadie in the will as guardian. We just don't think you're responsible enough to care for a child."

He looks at me.

Lilah says, "What child?"

Isaac pulls Lilah's face into his shoulder. He heads down to the basement bedroom. Lilah begins to wail, "I want my Mommy."

Dave and I are alone.

"You could take her to Disney World sometime," I say to Dave.

"Diane." He sighs. "I don't want to hear it right now."

"Fine. But what about our bet?"

"You won. You get Helga."

"That wasn't the bet."

Dave and I now embark on a staring contest. It's not fair though, because he is all folded up on the couch, and I'm out in the middle of the room, on display. So, of course I'm the first to glance at my feet. "What," I say.

"You know what," he says.

"No, what?"

"It's a fantasy. It's a game we play."

"It doesn't have to be."

"Diane." The staring is happening again.

"What."

He laughs. "Shut up with the whats already."

"You shut up."

"I'm going kayaking." He stands, picks up the lantern.

"But, Dave, wait, what."

He gives me a knuckle rub on the head, and he leaves.

My shoulder hurts and I press my hand to it. I sit on the couch until I'm sure it's quiet below, then I walk down to the bedroom. Isaac is reading in the armchair. Lilah is asleep. She's been scrubbed and re-jammied. She lies across the bed as if she threw herself there, her arms raised, her white nightgown twisted up to her waist, her face red and smeared from crying.

"She wanted you," he says, not looking up.

"Lilah's my hero," I say.

"We'll hire a tow truck in the morning."

"I'm going down to the dock for a while."

He looks up from the book with reassuring, sad eyes. "We've caused a great deal of damage, but we can fix this, Diane. And I'm not only talking about the car. We just need to work harder." He smiles. "No quitters allowed."

I stumble in the dark towards the water. I can hear

the quiet splash of Dave's paddle and see the lantern wink like a gold eye as it disappears around a bend.

I wonder if she's out there with him, but then I see her. She's naked, as usual, and sitting on the roof of the car, hugging her knees, gazing stiffly out to sea.

"Isn't that a little overdramatic," I call.

She doesn't answer. The little plastic things float and glow on the water.

I take off my clothes and wade in. The water is even warmer than the air. My toes sink into the sludge. I think of broken glass from the car wreck. I feel my way, on my toes, trying to test for the sharp edge of glass before it cuts me, then climb onto the submerged hood, all the butterflies scraping my knees. I pull myself onto the roof and sit beside her. I can feel the wings pressing into my butt. We're both slick with algae.

"Isaac's going to have it towed out in the morning," I say.

"He broke up with me," she says.

"He always does that."

"I guess you're the only woman he's ever loved," she says.

"I'm not a woman."

"That's a weird thing to say." She watches her toes.

I watch her. I imagine sliding my fingers all the way down. It would be prickly there, where she shaves. We'd be breathing hard, hardly acting, hardly holding back, so close to real.

She looks up. "What."

"I feel reckless tonight." I run my finger down her arm.

I know she's thinking about it, Dave and I could

be twins, and she could have me, she could recoup her losses. But she decides to recoup them in a different way.

"No, thanks," she says.

She slides off the car, and away.

It's late now. Lilah and Isaac—the light off from that window, Anna, somewhere, Dave, somewhere else. The moon is just a knife edge, the lake is green and still. A mosquito hovers near my ear, all in a passion for blood. Whining, No quitters allowed.

Miraculous Escapes
by Dave Tanaka

Welcome to Good Neighbor!
Choose a neighborhood: Bierce Park
Choose a category: Crime and Safety
Add subject: We're in this together!

Post message:
My name is James Nowicki, I'm a seventy-two-year-old
retired middle school assistant principal who has lived
in this neighborhood for forty years. I'm old enough to
have lived in this town before it was invaded by hippies
and marijuana tourists, the snowflake types that think
we need to keep this town weird as it says on the t-shirts.
But I know and you know that since the needle exchange
invaded our neighborhood we've seen our streets taken
over by crack addicts, tweekers, and panhandlers. How
many have posted about bicycle theft? How many posts
about stolen mail? Keyed cars? Garbage rifled through?
Dirty needles? Drug deals in the park and on the street?
I'm going to post each day for a month, a record of the
incidents I witness in our neighborhood, and present
the log at the next City Council meeting. I urge you to
do the same. We're in this together!

THANKS: 14

Choose a neighborhood: Bierce Park
Choose a category: Crime and Safety
Add subject: We're in this together!

Post message:
Log date: November 16

11:00 AM: Apparently white male, medium height/ build, UC Santa Cruz Slug sweatshirt, yelling obscenities in park across street, per usual. FU@@, COC@ SUCKER, etcetera, you've heard it. Pacing across entrance, per usual. For the hearing-impaired, this apparently strung out individual hollers in the park approximately three times a week. You know him as Señor Screamer. I go out on second floor balcony to document. Screamer screams, "I see you, Sir. Yeah, you, there on the balcony. Staring is very rude. It's rude to take photos of strangers." I continue to take photos, attached here, though blurry because distance. Screamer then screams, "Fuuu** you! Go ahead—call the cops again."

11:05 AM: I call the cops.

11:35 AM: Cops arrive (wonder of wonders). Talk to Señor Screamer. Screamer leaves park, heading towards Diane's Restaurant where he dumpster dives, as is his habit. Can someone at Diane's put a lock on that dumpster?

2:30 PM: School bus drops pupils off in front of park, per usual. Three apparently Hispanic males, ages approximately 8-9 years old, stuff candy wrappers into neighbor's "little library." I go to balcony, take photos of them. Yell down, "Pick up those wrappers." They scream, "El viejo diablo " (Google translation: little old devil man) and run toward Button Street.

2:35 PM: I call the cops, report incident.

3:00 PM: Cops have not responded, per usual.

3:15 PM: I descend, take time due to bum hip, arm myself with plastic bag and "trash grabber" ($6.47, Amazon Prime, you can read my review, three stars because tongs too sharp), exit house, open gate, cross street to neighbor's "little library" (an old glassed-in cabinet painted a glaring aqua plunked onto a post). I grab wrappers, deposit in bag. Open neighbor's gate, covered in multiple strings of bells, so jingle jingle jingle. Knock on door of this neighbor, a "writer" who "works" from home ("Writer" always takes morning tea on his porch in his pajamas and at five p.m. takes cocktail on porch, still in his pajamas, you've probably seen him on your way to and from actual work.)

Conversation:

Me: (holding out trash bag) "Three juvenile delinquents stuffed this trash in your 'little library' again."

"Writer": (apparently Asian male, apparently in his thirties, in pajamas, per usual) "Okay."

Me: "I've warned you before that your so-called 'little library' attracts vagrants."

"Writer": "Books attract vagrants?"

Me: "Have you been to the downtown library? It's basically a homeless shelter. Bierce Park Books is three blocks from here. You're probably hurting her business. Everyone needs to support local businesses. (NOTE: is that poor girl who runs the used bookstore on Good Neighbor? Somebody should tell her what's going on. Also, tell her to organize that store of hers, then maybe she'd have some customers.)

"Writer": (taking bag) "Thanks, Mr. Nowicki, I'll take care of it."

(NOTE: "Writer" is not on "Good Neighbor!" though I have invited him through email multiple times. I have looked "Writer" up on Amazon and he has one book of short stories published seven years ago, title: *Miraculous Escapes.* Only two reviews, both three stars, #3,053,049 ranking. He has placed two copies of his own book in his "little library," but apparently no one has ever taken it out. Apparently, no one has ever taken a book out of the little library at all, although he checks it daily. Am I right? Have any of you taken advantage of the "little library" or is it just a receptacle for trash?)

5:00 PM: "Writer," still in pajamas, exits house, puts on rubber boots he always leaves by door (despite my warnings that they will attract thieves), nails my plastic bag to fence beside "little library" with cardboard sign, "put trash here." Drinks cocktail on porch.

THANKS: 13

Choose a neighborhood: Bierce Park
Choose a category: Crime and Safety
Add subject: We're in this together!

Post message:
Log date: November 17

5:45 AM: Woken by bells on gate of "Writer's" house. Jingle jingle jingle. Part curtain. Individual in hoodie apparently young adolescent male caught in act of stealing "Writer's" rubber boots. I run downstairs (really gimp downstairs because of bum hip), take up trash grabber by door, exit house. Thief still in "Writer's" yard. I brandish trash grabber aloft from across street, yell: "Drop those boots." Thief does not drop boots. I limp across street, open gate, hit boots out of perpetrator's hands with trash grabber. I yell "Writer's" name because in rush forgot phone to call cops. Thief makes to attack me, but trips on fallen rubber boot, grabs onto trash grabber on way down. Mental. I yell "Writer's" name again.

"Writer": (exiting house, in pajamas, long hair loose like wild man of Borneo) "What's going on?"

Me: "Call the cops!"

"Writer" looks down. I look down. Thief's hood has fallen back, revealing an apparently mixed-race female, late teens or early twenties, short dark hair, multiple piercings and whatnot in ears and nose, one big brown eye, holding other eye with both hands. Blood seeping through fingers. Apparently hit trash grabber with eye.

Thief: "My eye, my eye. This old man attacked me."

Me: "I apprehended her stealing your rubber boots."

"Writer": (ignoring me, to thief) "Are you okay?"

Thief: "Something's wrong with my eye." Blood dripping down face onto sweatshirt (will definitely stain if not washed immediately).

"Writer": (dialing 911 on his phone) "We need an ambulance."

Me: "Are you mental? She's probably faking. Do you know how much an ambulance costs? Over a thousand dollars. Do you have insurance?"

"Writer": (finally paying attention, hangs up). "I'll drive you to the emergency room. My car's right here."

"Writer" helps Thief to feet. Half carries Thief to car (Prius, keyed on both sides). Drives away, silently, because Prius. Leaves rubber boots on sidewalk. I line them back up on his porch, ready to lure another thief.

10:00 AM: Prius returns. "Writer" goes around to passenger side door. Helps out Thief, who is wearing eye patch like pirate. "Writer" and Thief enter "Writer's" house.

11:10 AM: I am questioned by police. Officers P and S accuse me of assault with a weapon on private property.

Say I'm lucky "victim" not pressing charges. I express outrage. Officer P, apparently Hispanic, says, "Maybe you should choose your battles, Sir. You've called 911 twenty-two times in the past month." P and S smirk at each other. I express outrage that neighborhood has been allowed to become like in movie *Falling Down*. Question officers if they have even seen *Falling Down* with Michael Douglas. (You should rent it on Amazon Prime, $3.99, I gave it five stars—story of regular man fighting back against falling down neighborhood like ours.) Officer S asks me if I've seen *Rear Window*, his favorite movie. I ask officers if they are arresting thief. Officer S says, "You mean female victim?"

Are there any witnesses to what actually occurred at 5:45 AM? Private message me.

THANKS: 3

Choose a neighborhood: Bierce Park
Choose a category: Crime and Safety
Add subject: We're in this together!

Post message:
Log date: November 18, 2016

9:00 AM: "Writer" and Thief taking tea on front porch. Thief still wearing eye patch, bruise on cheek. Bruises easily due to drug use? 98% likelihood Thief is tweeker, will rob "Writer" blind, kill him in his sleep, etcetera. I am predicting this now. (I suggest some of you walk by and take some photos for evidence of this future crime. I don't want to reveal house number, but I'm sure you know the residence. The one with the overgrown front yard, jasmine and morning glories, etcetera choking everything, weeds growing onto sidewalk through the white fence which is broken off and tilting in places, front porch painted purple, that "little library" hammered onto a post by that gate with those bells all over it, generally doing his best to 'keep it weird.' This "Writer" is not your typical Santa Cruz hippie though, because Asian. "Writer" bought house 15 months ago. At first I thought he would help us save the neighborhood, because Asian. At my middle school Asian pupils were always best behaved, neatest handwriting, etcetera, but this "Writer" has long, shaggy hair that looks like birds could make nest in it. To describe "Writer," hard, because doesn't look like actor I can think of, because so few Asian actors, maybe like Bruce Lee if Bruce Lee wore a mop on his head to play a washed-up "Writer." More like pre-washed-up because never famous. I wish Bruce Lee lived in neighborhood, he'd keep everyone in line with his karate chops. Imagine his family bankrolls him, "Writer" not Bruce Lee. Probably his parents are immigrants who worked all their lives running a small business, a fortune cookie factory in Chinatown, to put him through the best schools, and this is how he repays them, living off their money pretending to write. Parents never visit, as far as I can see. Probably too busy at the factory. Probably better for them not to observe how he's living, probably give them heart attack.)

10:00 AM: Thief, still with eye patch, wearing "Writer's" large rubber boots, is weeding "Writer's" overgrown yard. So nabbed rubber boots after all.

11:00 AM: Still weeding. Has filled three trash bags with green waste. (Thief looks like that actress, from *High School Musical*, what's her name. Great movie, five stars. Just googled it: Vanessa Hudgens. Like Vanessa Hudgens playing thief/tweeker with eye patch. I wish Vanessa Hudgens lived next door, but just crazy dream because she would have moved out long ago due to crack addicts, etcetera.)

Noon: Thief examines "little library." Takes out *Babysitter's Club Mystery*. Makes me think. Either this book is much too young for thief or thief is much younger than first thought. Is thief a runaway? Situation suddenly takes on new, ugly light. Perhaps it is thief in danger from "Writer," not other way round. Did "Writer" put *Babysitter's Club Mystery* in "little library" to lure underage girls? Possibility of child pornography ring raises its depraved head. Consider calling cops, but will gather evidence first.

1:00 PM: With my copy of *An Occurrence at Owl Creek Bridge* I make my way to front gate of "Writer's" house. Shake gate with bells to get her attention. Call to thief, "If you're going to read which may strain your one eye and cause blindness, at least read a classic. Our park is named after the author."

She comes down off purple porch. Stands on other side of gate. Undernourished in ratty t-shirt, though no apparent needle marks on arms or signs of that popular cutting hobby either. Close up, she is not so much

Vanessa Hudgens, more like very pretty lollipop with long neck and round face with huge eye.

Thief: "You're a tough old geezer. You remind me of my grandpa."

Me: "Where is your grandfather?"

Thief: "Dead."

Me: "What about your parents?"

Thief: "Same."

Me: "How old are you?"

Thief: "How old are you?"

Me: "Seventy-two."

Thief: "You don't look a day older than seventy-one, ha ha."

Me: "Very funny. What is your name?"

Thief: "Peyton."

Me: "Peyton?"

Thief: "Peyton Fahrquhar." She spells it for me.

Me: "Why were you reading that babysitter book?

Thief: "I put it under the leg of a rickety chair."

Alert: See attached photo of Peyton Fahrquhar that I took from second floor balcony. Runaway in danger? If anyone recognizes her, private message me.

1:45 PM: Correction: Peyton is an alias. Realize from googling that the girl gave me the name of the main character in *Owl Creek Bridge*. Clever. Perhaps secret message. Peyton is being hanged at beginning of story, in grave danger, get it? Also through googling discovered that the author, Ambrose Bierce, disappeared. Maybe she is in danger of 'disappearing,' if you know what I mean, or maybe she has already disappeared so to speak, is escaping from some danger, hiding out. This person is clearly educated. Have strong feeling family is not all dead, and may be looking for her. This young person may be in danger from older pervert type.

1:50 PM: Decide to call cops. Express my concerns re: runaway, child pornography, etcetera.

3:11 PM: Officer P knocks on "Writer's" door. Peyton answers. Officer P speaks. Peyton takes out what appears to be an ID. Officer examines briefly and returns (could be fake). Officer P and Peyton look over at my house and laugh. I drop curtain.

5:00 PM: Peyton and "Writer" taking cocktails on purple porch. More laughter.

THANKS: 1

Choose a neighborhood: Bierce Park
Choose a category: Crime and Safety
Add subject: We're in this together!

Post message:
Log date: November 19

9:00 AM: Peyton is weeding again. Must admit Peyton is busy bee. Good work ethic. Perhaps of Hispanic origin?

10:00 AM: Now Peyton is fixing fence. Nailing loose pickets.

2:15 PM: Now Peyton is weeding sidewalk in front. Looks up, waves to me (on my second floor balcony).

Peyton: "How are you this morning, Mr. Nowicki?"

She is clearly exhausted from hard work. Where is that "Writer"? Probably snoozing away the day on his couch in his pajamas. Has gotten himself good deal. Beautiful underage handyman. Hot day even though November. You know. I make glass of Lipton iced tea and bring it to her. She thanks me. While we are both in yard, school bus stops in front of park, down street, per usual. Same three miscreants exit, backpacks bumping on their backs as they chase each other down street. We can see them easily because Peyton has clipped the hedge back. They see me. "El diablo," they scream and throw their wrappers in "Writer's" yard, begin to run away laughing. But then. Peyton hands me iced tea. Vaults the fence like superhero runs down the street after them. Next thing I know she is dragging two of them by the shirt back down the street.

Peyton: (giving them shove) "Pick it up."
They gather up wrappers.

Peyton: "Apologize to Mr. Nowicki."
They apologize. One is crying (younger one, maybe seven years old).

Peyton: "Do you accept their apology?"

Me: "Yes."

Peyton: "If I ever see wrappers in my yard again I am going to hunt you little fu**ers down and kill you. Get it?"
They nod. She lets them leave.
Peyton takes glass of tea back and finishes it.

3:30 PM: Note: Not sure what to think about this turn of events. What is your opinion?

4:00 PM: Note: Peyton said "my" yard.

5:00 PM: Peyton on porch drinking cocktail. "Writer" nowhere to be seen. Yard is spick and span, fence is fixed, but where is "Writer"? Not drinking tea this morning, not checking his "little library," not having his cocktail at five, per usual.

THANKS: 1

Choose a neighborhood: Bierce Park
Choose a category: Crime and Safety
Add subject: We're in this together!
Post message:
Log date: November 20

9:00 AM: Peyton chops up little library with axe. Peyton is expert with axe.

Peyton: (noticing me watching from balcony) "Hey, Mr. Nowicki, I know you hate this little library. It attracts scumbags, am I right?"

Me: I don't know what to say, so just take photo, attached here.

Peyton: "Got any more of that Lipton?"

9:30 AM: I bring tea out (excuse to gather info).

Me: "What does the "Writer" think of you getting rid of the 'little library'?"

Peyton: "I'm taking care of things now."

Me: "But he checked that little library every day."

Peyton: "Exactly. He needs a break."

Me: "I'd like a word with him."

Peyton: (repeating herself) "I'm taking care of everything

now."

Me: (not knowing what to say) "That's nice of you."
Peyton: "I'm not nice. I'm family."

Me: "What do you mean?"

Peyton sits down on purple porch, drinks tea, precedes to tell me long story. I can't quote the exact words. But here's a summary:
—she's "Writer's" sister! Half-sister. Older sister! (means Peyton must be at least in thirties, just has that Asian thing where don't age)
—her father and mother met in grad school, both library science, but pregnant mother had to quit.
—the father called Peyton's mother "The mistake."
—the father abandoned Peyton and mother, thought he could just erase them, pretend they never happened. Father became fancy head librarian at research university, married new woman, had a kid, a bookworm, the "Writer."
—broke first woman's heart. She never got over him.
—Peyton pretty much grew up in a library. Mother couldn't afford babysitter so she would hide Peyton in the stacks while she worked various unsavory jobs. But always tried to instill love of Japanese culture in Peyton. Like karate.
—Peyton bitter because both kids bookworms, but writer became a "writer," Peyton became a transient.
—After Peyton's mother died two years ago, Peyton tried to see father, but he rebuffed her, said wife didn't know about the first mistake, too late to start over,

etcetera. But Peyton said you can't escape the past and it's never too late to set things right.

Me: (after long story) "But why are you chopping down the library, then? If your mother loved libraries? If you're a bookworm?"

Peyton: "I never said I loved libraries. I said I grew up in libraries. It's kind of a love-hate relationship. More hate, if you know what I mean. Hiding away in books is just an escape, a way not to see, know what I mean? You and me, Mr. Nowicki, we got nothing to do but see."

Me: "But. You were stealing his boots."

Peyton: "It's a joke we like to play on each other."

Me: (Start to say, But you never met "Writer," but Peyton cuts me off)

Peyton: "I like you, Mr. Nowicki, you just want to stay connected, am I right? Maybe a little bored, a little lonely? I get it. You just want to keep your eye on things. If I didn't have that lemon tree in front of the window, you could see right into my house, couldn't you?"

THANKS: 1

Choose a neighborhood: Bierce Park
Choose a category: Crime and Safety
Add subject: We're in this together!

Post message:
Log date: November 21

9:00 AM: I pretend to check my mailbox. Peyton is power washing the Prius in front of "Writer's" house. No sign of "Writer." Suddenly, Peyton turns and looks at me. First time not wearing eye patch. The eye patch eye is different color, not brown but gold. One eye brown, one eye gold. Shocking. Google says it is called heterochromia. Perhaps wound and eye patch just ruse to hide deformity. Or identity.

11:00 AM: Screamer in the park. Peyton vaults gate again. Walks down the street to the park, right in, up to Señor Screamer, says something to him, he screams, "Fu$$ you, ma'am." Peyton does something with her hands, some kind of karate move maybe. Screamer screams in a different way, holds eyes. Peyton says something else. Screamer stumbles out of park, hands over eyes, not towards Diane's, towards the health clinic. Peyton walks back into house.

THANKS: 1

Choose a neighborhood: Bierce Park
Choose a category: Crime and Safety
Add subject: We're in this together!

Post message:
Log date: November 22

I haven't seen "Writer" in four days, not in the morning, not in the evening. No tea, no cocktail. Has anyone seen

"Writer"? Private message me if you have.

THANKS: 1

Choose a neighborhood: Bierce Park
Choose a category: Crime and Safety
Add subject: We're in this together!

Post message:
Log date: November 25

I've been doing some internet research. Found an interview of "Writer" in *Catamaran Literary Reader*. Interviewer asks "Writer" about origin of his story, "Rubber Boots." "Writer" says parents died in a fire two years ago. Suspected arson, but no one ever caught. All that was left: father's rubber boots on doorstep. Everything else burned. "Writer" used inheritance to buy house in Santa Cruz, etcetera. "Writer" says he is only child. I'm going to Bierce Park Books to see if I can get copy of his book on sale.

THANKS:

Choose a neighborhood: Bierce Park
Choose a category: Crime and Safety
Add subject: I am not a pervert!

Post message:
Log date: December 3

6:00 PM: First time I've been able to post since I've

been home from the hospital. I see someone has made Good Neighbors! take down all my posts. Please read this quickly before they take this one down, too. I am not a pervert. If you had been reading my log, you know I was and still am concerned for the well-being of my neighbor, the writer Dave Tanaka who lives or lived opposite me, because said writer has been missing since November 18th. I documented all of this, before it was erased. Did anyone take a screen shot? Private message me.

On the night of November 23rd at approximately 11 PM I donned black pants, didn't have black turtleneck but wore green. Giants baseball cap. I made my way downstairs, took long time because hip, per usual. Nobody on street as far as I could see because cold night, 42 degrees, cloudy. You remember. Very dark because city refuses to put up more lights on our street to deter criminals. Cross street to gate of writer's house. Worried about bells on gate, so open gate very, very slowly, inch by inch. Little jingle jingle jingle, but not much.

I freeze, wait.

Nothing.

Light on in downstairs of Dave's house. I hold onto branch of lemon tree, lemon tree sways. I freeze, wait, nothing. Then with help of branch I duck down, behind lemon tree, right up to front window. Peer in. Living room is lined with bookshelves, but bookshelves almost all empty. Peyton is boxing up books, boxes everywhere on floor. Drinking beer. And by back door? Four heavy duty green trash bags and next to them, leaning against back door, axe. I continue to watch (I realize now that

Peyton was in men's tighty-whities, no bra, definitely full-grown woman, but at the time I didn't notice because too busy documenting evidence of crime).

Then Peyton, as if with supernatural senses, looks up. Seems to stare right at me with those heterochromia eyes.

I freeze, wait.

Then she goes back to packing up books, humming and drinking beer. I grab branch, whole tree sways, don't even care because unnerved, duck under, come out from tree.

Peyton. Just standing there in hoodie, waiting for me. I scream. Peyton jabs me in the eyes, then turns her hand into a knife and whacks me in the neck. It hurts so much. I stumble around, can't see, can't breathe, trip over tree root or something, crash to ground. My hip on fire, now, too. Scream for help. Some of you came out, I'm sure, but I couldn't see. Did any of you video this? Next thing I know, ambulance. I'm screaming, "No, no ambulance," even though I have insurance, waste of money. I'm screaming, "She murdered him! She murdered him! Just look in the house!" Some of you must have heard me. I hear her telling the EMT's or the cops I was peeping in her window. That's all I remember, must have passed out.

Hip broken, surgery. Hazy, because drugged. Wake up at one point and there is Officer P, looming over me.

Me: "Did you search the house? Did you see the trash bags?"

Officer P: "You're a lucky man, Mr. Nowicki."

Me: "Lucky? I broke my durn hip."

Officer P: "Lucky because once again your neighbor is not pressing charges. You need to leave that young woman alone."

Me: "She's not my neighbor. She's not young. That's not her house. You have to listen to me. Read my posts on Good Neighbor! It's all there."

Officer P: "Mr. Nowicki, your neighbor, Dave Tanaka, is at this place called a writer's colony in upstate New York. He's left his house in the care of his sister. We've received an email from him."

Me: "But then, why is she throwing out all his books? What about the trash bags? Did you look inside?"

Officer P: "Mr. Nowicki, that's not your business. You're going to be laid up for a while, but after that, why don't you go on down to the Market Street Senior Center. They have folk dancing, ukulele lessons, wood carving. Great rehab for your hip. Something to do, meet people. Keep you out of trouble."

Now I'm stuck in a hospital bed in my own living room. Had a day nurse in, but she pulled the curtains down, said, "No more peeping, Mr. Nowicki."

Midnight: Alone, can't sleep, hip hurts, spooked. Light is

creepy because dern lavender scented candle nurse left, said house smelled musty. Keep hearing strange noises, but may be drugs. I keep thinking about this story in Dave Tanaka's book. It's called "Back in the Beginning, Dangerously Close to the End." It makes zero sense because it's about pilgrim times, but everyone knows no Asian pilgrims. I hate that story. It's like a secret message just for me—like, help me, help me, Mr. Nowicki. Read it, you'll see (I bought the only used copy at the bookstore, but kindle version .99 cents). The story also mentions Ambrose Bierce. On Google they say they called him Bitter Bierce back in the day because he was bitter. Did you know that Ambrose Bierce disappeared when he was exactly my age? Just disappeared into Mexico, worst place to disappear. At least he left his writing, but unless someone took screen shots, my writing is gone. None of you took screen shots, did you? I have come to the bitter realization that I am the only one who cares about the mysterious disappearance of Dave Tanaka (and probably Ambrose Bierce, too).

1:00 AM: You know what Ambrose Bierce's last words were? "As to me, I leave here tomorrow for an unknown destination." I just googled, and found five "writer's colonies" in upstate New York. One is by a lake. Very nice. I might just call a taxi, get myself to the airport, rent an RV in Albany, pay a little visit to those writer's colonies, take the law into my own hands as they say. Who's to stop me?

THANKS:

Choose a neighborhood: Bierce Park
Choose a category: Crime and Safety
Add subject: A sad day

Post message:
Hi everyone, I just joined Good Neighbor. My name is
Dave Tanaka. I'm writing from the east coast where I've
been at a writer's residency. I heard the sad news that
Mr. Nowicki is presumed dead. We're all sorry to lose
a respected neighbor and member of the community.
I wasn't able to go to the memorial, but my sister went
and told me two of his former students attended.

First off, I think we all need to thank the fire department
for keeping the fire from spreading to other houses.
I don't know what they are planning to do with the
remains of Mr. Nowicki's house, but my sister says that
it's an unsightly mess and a sad reminder, and I hope his
relatives or the city take care of this soon.

I heard from some of you that Mr. Nowicki had been
planning to visit me just before he died. If so, that's
touching. Who knows? Maybe he'll show up someday
to give me a piece of his mind...

I have a teaching opportunity here, so will be relocating,
but my sister will take care of everything at my house.
She has shipped me most of my books, and she's helping
me get rid of some extra things, some knickknacks, CDs,
a few paintings, so if you want anything, they will be in
boxes outside the house before she donates them all to
Goodwill on Monday. She's also going to start teaching

Karate lessons in the park on Mondays, Wednesdays and Saturdays. Stop by, she'll be watching out for you.

Back in the Beginning, Dangerously Close to the End
by Dave Tanaka

lderman had something hidden under a deerskin. He held out a small rabbit fur purse, and when he judged enough English shillings and Spanish coins had been stuffed into it, he slowly raised the deer's pale skin. Everyone crowded in to get a good look. In a jar of cloudy rum a human hand floated. Written on the jar were the words, *King Philip, his hand.*

Led by Captain Benjamin Church, Alderman had shot King Philip as he tried to escape from a swamp thirteen days earlier. They drew and quartered Philip, stuck his head on a pole in Plymouth, and rewarded Alderman with the moneymaking hand.

A military drumming soon announced the other attraction of the day, and Alderman lost his crowd. Six chained Narragansett men were lead out onto the newly built scaffold. The gaoler, a short, tubby man with a flare for the dramatic, adjusted his big black hat and cutlass importantly, and then made a great show of unlocking the chain and hauling it off while a soldier kept his musket at the ready should they think of escaping. Then the gaoler read out the crimes in an outraged voice: *trayterously, rebelliously royetousley and routously armed, weaponed and arrayed themselves with Swords, Guns and Staves, etcetera and have killed and bloodely murthred many of his*

majestys good Subjecys. The crowd jeered and booed, and
the drummer let loose a little flurry on the calfskin.

Unfortunately, the first five Narragansetts were
all dressed and shorn like Englishman. All fell to their
knees and prayed to the Great Father in good English.
One even said, Forgive them for they know not what
they do. They all died quietly. This muted the hilarity a
little. The last man up promised to be more exciting. He
looked like a real savage, and he was a minor celebrity to
boot: one of the principal warriors behind this Indian
uprising, brother-in-law to King Philip, so recently
vanquished. He was tall, had only half a head of hair,
and was completely naked except for a scrap of leather
between his legs. Quinnapin said nothing as they yanked
the rough rope around his neck and tightened it.

The minister beside him asked if he desired to pray.
The crowd waited, hoping at least for a savage growl or
war cry, but Quinnapin looked over their heads, as if
he were waiting for someone. His tied-together hands
clenched and unclenched behind him. Then Quinnapin
noticed Alderman in his yellow shirt, holding the jar
with Philip's hand inside. Alderman—his childhood
friend. Once swimming together, they ran their hands
along the rubbery flank of a seal.

The minister repeated his question: a last prayer?
The goaler tapped his foot. The crowd began to talk to
each other.

Quinnapin looked at Alderman, just one more time,
but it was the kind of stare that causes milk to sour,
chickens to stop laying eggs, the kind of look that gives
babies colic, that sends bad luck nipping at the heels for
years, not because it was so furious, but because it was
so full of looking. Alderman hid the jar under the skin.

Nervous about losing his audience, the goaler shoved Quinnapin over the hole. He stumbled, couldn't right himself with his hands tied, and fell, his feet scraping over the platform after him. The rope wasn't tight enough to break his neck, or his dragging feet lessened the force of his fall. Quinnapin choked loudly. He struggled to get his hands free. His legs swam in air.

There was still time for someone to offer assistance. Perhaps Susan Hutchinson stood in the crowd, there for a visit with her sister Bridget, who lived on Aquidneck. Susan was the daughter of Anne Hutchinson, the American Jezebel who was banished from Boston for interpreting the Bible. Anne Hutchinson believed in friendship with all people, and moved to the New Netherlands outback with her seven youngest children. They made a home between the Dutch and the Siwanoy. Then, the Dutch massacred eighty Siwanoy women and children. The Siwanoy sent a message to Anne and told her there would be retaliation—leave the area and avoid harm. But Anne trusted in God and good neighbors. The Siwanoy massacred Anne Hutchinson and her children, all but small Susan, who was discovered hidden in the cleft of a rock. The chief of the Siwanoy, Wampage, changed his name to Anne to honor Anne Hutchinson and adopted Susan as his daughter. Susan lived for eight years with the Siwanoy before she was ransomed, some say against her will. Now she may have stood with her English husband and ten children, watching Quinnapin choke, thinking about her parents Anne and Anne, both lost to her, but if she was, she also remained silent, her hands fluttering at her neck.

Or perhaps one of the Quakers in the crowd would remember that it was Quinnapin's grandfather,

Canonicus, who gave all this land to Roger Williams so that they could worship as they pleased and not be hung for it by the Puritans. Perhaps a Quaker would cry out for mercy.

Quinnapin had gotten his hands loose now and was struggling to pull the rope from his neck. He should stop trying to yank the rope off his neck. He should grab the rope above his head and hoist himself up. He can't get his fingers under the rope. It's too tight. He needs help.

What about time travel? Not the Ambrose Bierce all in your head kind. The blockbuster time travel kind where there is a sudden flash of light and a Special Ops serviceman lately deployed in Iraq or Afghanistan suddenly finds himself on the scaffold. Maybe he's a descendent of the people who are hanging Quinnapin, or maybe he's a descendent of Quinnipin's people, or both, either way he belongs to the people of last chances and miraculous turnarounds, so he knows what to do. He employs his special karate chops and amazing defensive moves. Wack, wack, chop, kick, they have no idea what hit them. The Coatmen all go flying off the wooden platform, who even knows or cares if they're dead or alive. He ties one of those bullshit candy-ass muskets into a knot and it fires on the self-important guy who's holding it. Then he cuts the noose with his knife, and he and Quinnapin leap off the stage and hightail it out of town. They run through blueberry scrub and over rocks until they come up against a high cliff, but they don't hesitate, they leap. Seems like there's no way they can make it, flying and falling at the same time, their arms windmilling, they hit the ocean, disappear.

But they rise. They rise. They're swimming together, the Indian and the savior of Indians, they grin, toss their wet hair. It sparkles in the sun.

Quinnipin's body began to spasm violently. Perhaps the jerking would cause the rope to break, it was possible, it had already been weakened by the five men before him. Nooses had broken before. The noose broke for the son of one of King Philip's warriors at the beginning of the war. The boy watched his father die, but then the rope tore for him. They let the boy go. It happened.

Quinnipin's hands dropped from his neck. His legs were still shivering though, so he was alive, so there was still time.

But not here. I'm sorry, not here.

Breathing Room

Diane's first thought upon waking is of her. Her daughter's karate teacher always says, First thought, best thought. And maybe it is the most Buddhist of thoughts, because it is not about desire, or the quelling of desire, not yet. Here at six-thirty in the morning, it's just the round face and then those eyes that have unbalanced her.

This is how it is from ten-thirty until noon: a slow build toward euphoria. They are biking together into town, and Diane realizes that she has everything she requires. Her sixteen-year-old daughter Lilah, with her own furious needs. Her husband Isaac, who has blue eyes, for whom she is necessary in a thick, muffled way.

They're on their way to Lilah's karate lesson in Bierce Park. At the beginning of the class Lilah stands in a clot of other teenagers who strut and hunch and talk self-consciously in that growly way they do.

Then Lilah is up and center. She's being tested today for her purple belt, and Diane is supposed to take pictures of the form, but she forgets because she is so busy watching this, this best moment of her week, this moment when her gaze is not pulled in two directions. There's just Diane's eyes on Lilah and her teacher as they move together, as Lilah drops her adolescent awkwardness, becomes someone else. Knife hand. Cat stance. Their twinned precision, doubled grace, how can they understand the edges of their bodies so completely? Diane wants that.

Isaac pats Diane's leg. Maybe it's enough. It is enough, when you add in the other love. Maybe it never gets better than this—any change at all and everyone might lose their balance.

Afterwards her daughter's sensei, who has one brown eye and one golden eye, ties the purple belt around Lilah's waist and says, "You can be any size you want to be, big or small, strong or weak, you choose. That's karate."

While Lilah's friends congratulate her, and Diane unlocks the bikes, she hears a little boy ask the sensei, What's wrong with your eye? The sensei smiles and asks the boy if he knows about kitsune, spirit foxes. She says kitsune can generate fire with their tails. They are tricksters, shapeshifters. They can even transform into humans. "You will know them by their golden eyes. And their bite." The little boy runs to his parents. Diane risks a quick look up and the teacher smiles a tiny, amused smile at her, like all the layers of this joke are shared between them. Diane remembers a story from the Bible, something about lighting foxes' tails on fire and letting them loose in fields of grain.

By noon they are at a restaurant, waiting in line, and something begins to edge into her heart. Suddenly she is thronged by absence. It's her choice, she reminds herself, she can be happy if she chooses, but her heart won't stop.

Isaac notices immediately. What's wrong?

Nothing.

I thought things were better. Things have been better for a long time.

They have been.

How can they talk? Lilah is right there, texting but also listening.

Her husband leaves and returns with two tulips and two small chocolate hearts covered over in red foil for Lilah and Diane.

He says, A lot of women like flowers and chocolates.

Lilah rolls her eyes, pleased, and snaps a photo of the flowers and chocolates for her Instagram. Diane says, "Thanks," but this gesture is wasted on her.

Biking out of the city is just about body, breath and sweat. She is as thoughtless and efficient as a mortar and pestle.

At home, Lilah says, "I'm outta here," and takes off on her bike.

Diane undresses for a shower.

Her husband says he wants one, too.

She says, "After me."

He says, "Why are you holding your towel so close?"

"I'll just be a second."

His face curdles. "It's okay," he says.

The shower is unbearably hot, but she cannot steam the feeling out. Afterwards, she tries the bedroom, even closes the door, but there is nowhere in the house that she can be. Nothing is her own, not the phone, not the computer, not even paper and pen.

She says she's going out for an hour or two, and Isaac gives her this look, you would cry for him if you saw that look, but she does not cry. She opens the door, walks out, closes it, and thinks, Maybe I'm a monster.

Maybe she is. Monster: 1) an organism formed of various animals in combination, like a centaur or griffin. 2) anyone grotesquely deviating from the normal shape or character. 3) anything with abnormal form or structure.

She's by herself now, so the rest of the story can come. It starts with that impossibly small smile that is an opening to everything else. And those long-fingered hands, those hands might kill her with their gentle insistence, their ruthless specificity.

Diane had a dream once, of drinking the sweat off a god. She'd always adored her elusive brother, and she originally thought the dream was about him, but Diane was wrong. The dream was about her. She's a five-foot-two karate teacher who grew up in libraries and trailer parks, a vegan who drinks cheap beer and chews tobacco, an orphan who scares children and claims her favorite books are *The Baby-Sitter's Club Mysteries*. Plus, Diane had this god dream years ago, before she met her, but still. The dream is about her.

So this is Diane now. True, Diane had always carried her brother around like a phantom limb, but there was the wife part and the mother part, they fit together, more or less, two symmetrical halves, the double arms, the two legs, etcetera, she pretty much had it all in working order. Until this other part emerged, this burning tail.

The Comeback Tour

When Isaac's wife was forty-four she decided she wanted to study karate. "It's never too late to change," Diane said. Isaac admired this forward thinking, which was not characteristic of her, and so was a small change in itself, even though the only exercise Diane had done previously was lifting sauté pans at her Michelin-starred restaurant. They'd already paid a small fortune to the karate teacher for five years of Saturday classes for their daughter Lilah, but Diane insisted on three private lessons a week. She started coming home saying things like "first thought, best thought" and talking about eating less meat, the kinds of things Diane would have mocked mercilessly in the past. Another small change. After six months of the karate lessons Diane left Isaac for their daughter's karate teacher, who was a woman.

Which was too much change, at least for Isaac.

Isaac thought of himself as forward-thinking, too, not so much in a transformational way, more in a ditch digging, plow horse kind of way, but definitely someone who still knew how to have fun. Examples of his fun side: he drank eight ounces of strong French Roast in the morning before he switched to decaf for the rest of the day; he drank a beer when he got home from work; and he had a long hot bath every weekend. He could be chill, as they say.

"It's not magic," he had always told his daughter, Lilah. "You can have whatever you want if you just work hard enough." But now, though he'd never slacked off, never, this divorce thing had happened. A setback. In fact, one could say that he was losing a serious chunk of what he'd worked for—his wife, his house, and the gourmet dining. But the point is, Isaac thought, the point is that it doesn't matter what the point is, you just have to dust yourself off and keep on keeping on. As his Grandpa Albert always said, "No quitters allowed!"

In August, they sold the house and most of their furniture. In September, Isaac and his seventeen-year-old daughter Lilah moved out of the suburbs into a small two-bedroom rental in the city across from Bierce Park. (Diane had announced that it would be best for Lilah to stay with Isaac, for stability in her last year of school.) Diane and her beloved sensei moved seventy miles up the coast to Pacifica into a wood and glass house on the ocean. Isaac bought a used Hyundai and furniture from Goodwill. He spent weekends fixing the furniture up, painting the wicker rocker, sanding and staining the coffee table. He found it satisfying—his furious conflict with the chipped brown paint on the coffee table—the way it yielded to his scraper in long, rubbery strips.

He thought he might be allergic to that stain though, because his face began to sting and burn around the edges, as if it were framed in nettles. Also, his eyes felt like there was grit in them, pretty much all the time. But he figured he'd ignore it, and it would go away.

Without his wife's ridiculously elaborate meals to come home to, he had more time to concentrate on his job as the County Director of Manpower—'We raise productivity!' He got home at nine or ten p.m., ate something, a defrosted bagel maybe, but mostly TV dinners, in front of the television. Frozen dinners! So tidy and compact, the satisfying peel of the plastic and then the steam rising, the creamed chicken and broccoli sharing the same comforting consistency and salty tang as the cherry crumble. A guy at work suggested he try meditation, so he bought a yoga mat to do relaxation exercises during his lunch hour, but he usually forgot and just worked straight through. Sometimes he worked so late, he slept overnight on his mat under the desk, got up, swiped on some deodorant and started working.

He was on his feet again. Really. Of course, it didn't help that his daughter, Lilah, didn't seem to want to be part of the solution. First, Lilah refused to change schools, and rode her bike seven miles back into the suburbs every morning. Bent furiously over her yellow beach cruiser, her books in a wicker picnic basket bungeed to the back, Lilah looked a little like the wicked witch in *The Wizard of Oz*. Except absurdly pretty, like her mother, with blond hair wisping out of a careless bun.

In the beginning of October, Lilah told him she wasn't going to college. She was going to Stone Turtle Cooking School in Maine. Isaac tried to be supportive, but he privately noted that Lilah had chosen her mother's profession and that the school was as far away as she could get and remain in the continental U.S. Lilah quit karate, which of course made Isaac happy, but then she obtained a part-time job as a caterer. She became an obsessive watcher of that cooking channel. It was hard not to think she was doing it for spite. Every time Isaac walked into the house the television assaulted him with culinary words—rough cut, mis en place, fine dice, harmony of flavors. It was unbearable. There was also something about how still she sat, Lilah, on the couch, her mouth hanging just slightly open, inviting flies, her long, spidery arms sagging at her sides, but eyes secretly alert, watching Isaac's every move. It made Isaac want to yell, What?

What Lilah complained about constantly was that there was nothing to eat in the house. Isaac told her to microwave the frozen food he'd stocked up on, which was convenient and lasted forever.

One day near the end of October, Lilah harassed Isaac into grocery shopping. They bickered over what to buy. Isaac was sure all those fresh vegetables would rot and go to waste. Lilah followed Isaac down the frozen food aisle, reading aloud the sodium content of the dinners he put in the cart. They were in line at the checkout when Lilah gave him a look straight out of a horror movie. "What is that?" Lilah hissed. She turned her back to Isaac and stared at the tabloid rack.

"What is what?" Isaac read one of the headlines out loud: "Chicken Pox Vaccine Transforms Child into a Monster."

Lilah snuck another look at him, then grabbed the tabloid and opened it in front of her face. "In your eye, Jesus, in your eye."

Isaac put his finger behind his glasses, swiped, and came away with something nasty.

"It's like there's a maggot in your eye," Lilah said behind the tabloid.

So, Isaac made a doctor's appointment. But instead of his regular doctor, Joyce, who they'd all been seeing since Lilah was born, a pale, skinny woman dressed in black under her white lab coat shouldered open the examination room door where Isaac sat on the table in one of those gowns. Isaac crossed his arms. "Is Joyce okay?" he asked.

The doctor didn't look up from her iPad. She started sneezing violently, one-two-three-four-five. Then she sighed, wiped her nose with a tissue, said in a smoker's voice, "Joyce has gone down to part-time. I'm Doctor Lucille—Joyce and I will be sharing the practice." She sneezed again, then reached out her knobby wrist to grab more tissues, still without taking her eyes from the iPad. "Don't worry, it's allergies. They've been acting up. The universe is attacking me."

"Good for Joyce," Isaac said.

Dr. Lucille swiped around on her iPad. "I see you've recently had an IUD removed. What are you using for birth control now?"

"What?"

Dr. Lucille finally looked at him, then swiped around some more. "Sorry, that's your wife's file. Same last name."

Isaac reminded himself about no quitters and keeping on. "I'm here because I think I am having some kind of reaction. Maybe a food allergy. Do you think I could have developed an allergy to frozen dinners?"

"What are you and your wife using for birth control?"

Isaac stared at the large diagram of a breast on the wall. "My wife and I separated over the summer. She's with a woman now."

"I can top that. My best friend, who also happened to be the nurse practitioner at my former practice, stole my husband. That's why I changed offices. Welcome to the pain that keeps on giving, am I right?"

"I like to think of divorce as an opportunity."

"Oh, are you on Tinder or one of those? I tried that and let me tell you I'd rather have surgery sans anesthesia, you know what I mean? But if that's your choice, you'll need to practice safe sex. I'm talking condoms, condoms, condoms."

"I don't have time to date. I'm not interested in all that."

"Have you tried anti-depressants?" the doctor asked, searching her iPad.

"My problem is that my eyes are infected, and my face burns all the time."

Dr. Lucille came closer, peered into his eyes with a penlight, asked him to look this way and that, pressed around the lids with her long fingers. She turned away a couple of times to sneeze. Then she wrote something on the iPad. "You have blepharitis. Your tears are thick and sluggish, prone to block the ducts and cause infection." She looked up. "Are you of Ashkenazi Jewish descent?" she asked.

"Yes," Isaac said. "What does that—"

"Because you appear to have rosacea, too. A swelling of the blood vessels in the face that causes redness and a burning sensation. Blepharitis and rosacia often present together. I'm not going to lie to you, it's not curable and it's almost definitely going to get worse."

Isaac remembered his great aunt with her red bulbous clown nose and weeping eyes. "Oh, well," he said.

"Common triggers are stress, hot drinks, alcohol and hot baths. You'll have to give up all that."

"Whatever, right?" Isaac smiled.

"That's aggressive." The doctor blew her nose hard. "Excuse me?"

"That. That 'whatever.' That's aggressive. I hate that. I moved here five years ago from New York, and I can tell you all that 'hang ten' and 'chilling out' is just a defense mechanism."

Isaac looked down at her rubbery black platform shoes, said carefully, "But don't you think wearing black and being sarcastic is a defense mechanism, too?"

The doctor sneezed.

After the appointment, Isaac went to the pharmacy to pick up the prescriptions, then back to work and stayed until eleven p.m. As he climbed the stairs to his apartment he saw the blue glow of the television through the window, thought, Cooking Channel, and steeled himself, but when he opened the door he heard Michael Jackson singing *Billy Jean*. There was a prince sitting on the couch with his daughter who was dressed in a tiny black flapper dress. They were holding hands. The prince wore a golden crown at a rakish angle on his black hair, a gold brocade jacket, gold tights and purple pointy velvet shoes.

Halloween. Of course, he knew it was the Halloween season, he wasn't that out of it, he'd noticed all the decorations around the office, he just hadn't put together that this was the exact particular night. "Happy Halloween!" Isaac said and stood behind them.

There he was on TV, the King of Pop before he'd finished construction of his mask—still darkish, with a realish nose, moonwalking. "He was a genius," Isaac said.

"He's a freak," Lilah said, but Isaac wasn't sure if Lilah was talking about him or the King of Pop.

"And who do we have here?" Isaac asked politely.

Lilah mumbled, "This is" somebody or other.

Isaac couldn't catch the name. It sounded like curling iron.

Prince Curling Iron turned and grinned. He was tall and thin, probably Indian.

"Are you a friend from school?" he asked, smiling back.

He said he was taking a "gap" year, but that he and Lilah worked for the same caterer. He wanted to be a chef, too.

"So, a cradle robber," Isaac said cheerfully.

Lilah gave him a quick, poisonous glance, maybe checking to see if he had pus in his eye, then went back to the television.

Isaac stood behind them. The *Thriller* dance sequence came on. Dressed all in red, that single curl on his forehead, so smooth in his transformation into whatever it was he was turning into. No one could move like him. "I used to do the *Thriller* dance when I was in college," Isaac said.

Lilah snorted.

"Memories," the prince said.

Isaac kept standing there, kind of bopping and mumbling along, *"There ain't no second chance against the thing with forty eyes, girl,"* until Lilah turned around and looked at him. Then Isaac said, "I want six inches between you at all times," trying to be funny but set limits at the same time. Lilah shivered her head and shoulders like someone had walked over her grave. "Curfew is midnight, even if you're home," Isaac said.

He kept checking back in every ten minutes or so, pretending to get a glass of water or opening and closing the refrigerator.

"There's nothing in there," Lilah announced sharply. "Nothing that's not frozen solid."

The next day was Saturday, but instead of taking a hot bath, Isaac scrubbed out his eyes with baby shampoo, held a warm washcloth to them for ten minutes, rubbed the antibiotic ointment on them, then covered his face in a clear prescription film, drank hot water and went to the office to get ahead on paperwork. He focused on his tasks, despite his burning face and itchy eyes, because the prescription said it could take up to five weeks to work.

Isaac came home to an empty house. He stood there for a minute, blinking to ungum his eyes, listening, but there was nothing to hear. He decided the whole place needed a brisk cleaning, so he beat up the kitchen floor with the broom and then started right to work on the couch, pounding those cushions. When he pulled one of them up he found something.

It was a small, glass blown pipe for marijuana. Milky glass with green and gold filament wound inside it. He held it in his palm. Weirdly, it still felt warm, like a little heating pad.

He put the cushion back and sat down. He couldn't

help thinking that purely objectively the pipe was cool looking. When he was in college they smoked out of homely, squat brown clay or wooden pipes or even a couple times an apple and tinfoil. Not that he had smoked a lot, just occasionally, on weekends. Isaac tried to remember the last time he'd been high. Maybe at that dance party he had just told Lilah about. It must have been the early nineties, his last year of college. He and Diane had danced the *Thriller* dance for hours, laughing and laughing.

Sitting on the couch, Isaac shrugged a little, *Thriller*-style, to make himself smile. They had been drinking ouzo jello shots that Diane had made. It was around that time that Diane's beloved younger brother who was always by her side like an f'n' bodyguard, a real cockblocker, a total a-hole actually, had dropped out of college, and Isaac had taken his place as her friend without benefits. He and Diane had been dressed as zombies that night, ripped things, sort of like Madonna/David Bowie zombies. Nail polish, hair jelled up. They smoked pot, he coughed a lot. And then she'd suddenly kissed him, just like that. Magic. That had been a fun time. He had always liked the smell of pot.

Isaac raised the pipe up. The bowl just held some burnt residue. He sniffed. A gold cloud rose out of the bowl. Then, like a giant powder puff, he felt it fluff onto his face. Something shot up into his nose and eyes like a super-sized portion of wasabi. His eyes watered. He began sneezing uncontrollably. Heat radiated across his cheeks and forehead, then into his mouth. His tongue felt numb, as if he'd eaten Szechuan pepper, then the heat went down his throat, pulsing into his chest and out through his arms. His fingers tingled.

Isaac stumbled into the bathroom and looked in the mirror. His entire face was covered in a fine, sparkling gold dust, gold like pan-for-gold, fairy dust, Oscars, disco-fever gold. Steady, he told himself. He turned the faucet on and splashed water on his face, over and over. Like sixteen times, golden water swirling in the drain. His mouth tasted funny. He touched his tongue to the inside of his cheek and swore he tasted licorice. He gargled with mouthwash three times. He was breathing heavily, squeezing and unsqueezing his eyes. He felt dizzy.

He heard Lilah come into the house. Isaac picked up the pipe from the bathroom vanity. He cleared his throat, checked himself in the mirror and went into the kitchen. Lilah was standing at the counter eating little puff pastry leftovers from her catering gig. "Surprise," Lilah said. "No food again."

Isaac held out the pipe on his palm. "What was in this?" he asked.

Lilah sneered. "I'm guessing weed."

"Where did you buy the pot?"

"Oh my god, of course you assume that. And BTW: it's called weed. Point is, there's no food." She pulled open the refrigerator. "There's nothing here. I can't live on day-old appetizers. You're starving me to death on purpose, aren't you? You want me to disappear!" She waved her hands in Isaac's face.

"Microwave something. And don't change the subject. I'm not going to lose it. I just want to know what was in this pipe? I found it in the couch. There was something gold, some substance I've never seen before.

What is it?"

"Okay, Dad, first of all, did it ever occur to you for one second that you bought that couch at Goodwill? I told you not to do that. It was probably owned by a stoner, or a dealer or even a drug lord who's going to come looking for the cash he stashed inside it. Or, maybe it was Mom's pipe. She's going through some pathetic midlife thing, right? Now, can we get back to the main point? If you want to continue life as a cyborg and basically desist from your parental duties, go right ahead, but I'm still an actual like, real human being with basic needs, so why don't you just leave me grocery money each week on the counter. You don't even have to see me, and I'll buy my own food and do my own cooking, and I'll graduate and be gone before you know it and then you can do your night of the living dead thing 24/7. Deal?"

"Your mother does not smoke pot. And she's never even sat on that couch."

"Stop obsessing about that stupid pipe. And stop calling it pot, it's weed, okay, weed!" Lilah grabbed the pipe out of Isaac's hand and threw it out the open window.

The broom was right next to Isaac so he hit Lilah over the head with it, the nylon brush part of course, not the handle, which wasn't satisfying at all, but still Lilah got dust all over her face.

Before Isaac could apologize, Lilah starting screaming, "I hate you so fucking much" and winging the puff pastry rounds at Isaac, pelting him on the face and chest, his t-shirt and face smearing with cream cheese and bright pink bits of lox. It stunk of lox, too, a smell Isaac couldn't stand.

"Screw this!" Isaac yelled. He charged into his room and slammed the door. He was gasping, and his face burned. He wondered if he was having a severe rosacea attack. He heard the front door slam. He wrestled his disgusting smelling shirt over his head and threw it on the floor. A glob of salmon and cream cheese dropped out of his hair.

Then he started sprouting tears. Involuntarily, like a medical condition. Like a sprinkler, soaking him. Maybe an effect of the blepharitis. He wiped his eyes. His tears were flecked with gold. He pulled his wallet off his dresser, dug into it and pulled out all his cash—sixty dollars. He crumpled the bills into an envelope, wrote 'grocery money' on the front, stomped out to the kitchen in his boxers and slammed the envelope on the counter. Then he stomped back into his room.

Standing in the middle of his bedroom, he suddenly felt more exhausted than he'd ever remembered feeling in his life. He climbed into his bed, still leaking tears, but he figured that was good, washing his eyes clean. He curled up and closed his eyes, even though he never took naps. He could have sworn the tears that leaked into his mouth tasted like ouzo. Isaac slipped into a thick, dreamless sleep.

When he awoke, he felt rested. Calm. No wonder, it was Sunday morning, nine a.m.—he had slept eighteen hours. Isaac smelled something baking and went into the kitchen. There was a grocery bag on the counter. Lilah was pulling blueberry muffins out of the oven. Without comment, Lilah put a muffin on a plate on the table, along with the butter dish and a knife. Then she started scrubbing the tin in the sink.

Isaac sat down. The muffin steamed when he broke open its pale yellow middle. Lilah had glazed the top with something lemony. The lemon tang and the blueberry's sweetness waltzed around his mouth. "I'm sorry I hit you with the broom," Isaac said. "I was freaked out because, I know this will sound strange, but by mistake I inhaled something that must have been inside the pipe, this sparkly gold dust. It got inside my mouth and eyes."

Lilah stopped scrubbing. "Are you serious? Jesus, Dad, who knows what was in there?"

"So, it really wasn't yours or Prince Curling Iron's?"

"Why are you calling him that? I told you his name is Vivaan."

"Right, Vivaan."

"And I'm like the only teenager in town that doesn't smoke weed. I hate that feeling, like I'm in a space suit. I just want to deal with reality." Lilah dried her hands. "Anyway, you need to go to the doctor's, like, now. Immediately. Why didn't you tell me? I never would have thrown away the stupid pipe. We should try and find it so they can analyze it or whatever."

"I feel fine now."

"You always say that, Dad. We're going to go look for it."

"Okay," Isaac said.

Still eating his muffin, Isaac followed Lilah out of the apartment and around the back where they'd never been. There was a high, rotting wooden fence with only about four feet between it and the building. The whole space was taken up with brambles and bushes.

"There's no way we can get in there," Isaac said. "But check this out, rosemary!" Isaac broke off a stem.

"How would you describe that smell?" Isaac asked. "It's like the smell of a fairytale." He handed it to Lilah. "And here's bay leaves. God, smell that, it's almost like cinnamon, but not."

Lilah held the rosemary and the ripped leaf in her fist. Her face twisted all around. "Sorry," she said.

"I'm sorry, too."

"But you still have to go to the doctor. Now."

Lilah's care, even if a little rough, made Isaac's eyes fill with tears again, and he turned away because Lilah had never seen him cry, especially gold tears.

Isaac went to urgent care. When the receptionist said, "Reason for visit?" Isaac didn't know what to say: "I might have possibly taken the wrong medication."

The receptionist looked up. "Do you have the medication you took with you?"

"No, it got thrown away." Isaac filled out the forms, waited a long time, paging through magazines. He surreptitiously ripped out a rosemary lamb recipe for his daughter, covering the ripping sound with a cough, though he never did anything like that, never. Finally, they called his name, and he went into the exam room and waited, staring at another diagram of another giant breast.

When the doctor came in it startled him a little, how attractive she was. Tall, dark curly hair, distractingly wide hips, with an absurdly shiny smile. "So, you may have taken the wrong medication?" She had a gentle voice and a perfume that smelled like grapefruit.

"It's a little complicated." He explained to her as simply as he could.

"I see. You snorted marijuana."

104

"Not on purpose. Seriously."

"Do you have the pipe?"

"No, I threw it away. Well, actually my daughter threw it away. It's complicated."

"Did you experience any symptoms afterward?"

"I felt a little dizzy and—emotional. I had a strange taste in my mouth. But all that could have been anxiety, I guess."

She checked his throat and eyes, blood pressure and pulse. "You seem fine. If you inhaled a small amount of marijuana it shouldn't hurt you."

"There's just one more complication. It was golden. The pot, or weed, I mean."

She looked interested. "How gold was it?"

"Glittery."

"Interesting. I believe there is a strain of marijuana actually called 24 Karat Gold. It's purported to smell and taste like tangerines."

"This tasted more like ouzo."

"There's several strains that taste like licorice."

"You know a lot about this pot stuff," Isaac smiled.

She smiled back. "Just a medical interest. I prescribe medical marijuana," she said. "For the relief of pain."

She got busy with his form. "Now, you've written here that you have acute cases of both rosacea and blepharitis."

"Yes, because I'm one of the chosen people."

She pressed beneath his eyes, shone a light in. When she ran the slightly scratchy pads of her fingers lightly over his face, he closed his eyes. "I see no sign of blepharitis or rosacea at all. Your eyes are absolutely clear, tear ducts not blocked. Your skin looks remarkably healthy—it has the elasticity of a thirty-year-old."

He realized his skin didn't burn. Nor his eyes. He blinked. He touched his face. "Weird."

"Sometimes these things are cyclical, they flare up, go away mysteriously. Maybe it was stress-related."

"Maybe the pot cured me." Isaac laughed nervously. "Weed."

"Do you smoke marijuana regularly?" she asked.

"Oh, no, never. The last time I smoked pot was at a Michael Jackson *Thriller* party in college."

"I love *Thriller!*" she said.

"You do?"

"*It's close to midnight!*" She shuffled forward a little, shuffled back.

"*And something evil's lurking in the dark!*" he sang. He jerked his head to his shoulder.

"*Under the moonlight,*" she jerked her head back at him.

"*You see a sight that almost stops your heart.*"

They smiled at each other.

"I'm actually having a *Thriller* party," Isaac said suddenly. "A big one. Next weekend. Next Saturday night at nine in fact. You should come. You can bring your husband."

"No husband," she said. "Do I need a costume?"

After the appointment, Isaac went to work, but at five he received a call. "Dinner will be served at seven p.m.," his daughter said gruffly.

"Oh, sweetie, I have a lot of work," Isaac said.

"Hello? It's Sunday." Lilah hung up.

Isaac went back to his Excel spreadsheet, but the glare from the window was on his screen. He went over to pull down the blinds. He stared at the golden, low-angled light. It was full of water somehow, tiny drops. He looked through the fine mist up into the blue sky. In fact, everything looked so bright and sparkly that he wondered if the blepharitis had been acting like a scrim. Then, for no good reason, Isaac packed the canvas bag he used for a briefcase, put on his jacket and left work, right then, at five.

When he got into the house it smelled so familiarly of garlic and onion simmering in butter that he had to stop in the doorway and make his face very still so he wouldn't cry. Aftereffects of his condition he assumed. Then he walked into the kitchen. His daughter and Prince Curling Iron stood side by side chopping vegetables at the counter, both in sweatshirts and jeans. The prince turned and smiled at him and said, "He's here." Lilah didn't smile but she went to the fridge, pulled out a beer and poured him a big glass. "It's Dragon's Breath IPA," she said. "Local. Everyone drinks craft beer now."

Isaac put his bag down and took off his jacket. He sat at the kitchen table and leaned his head up against the wall.

He sipped his beer. The window was open, and he swore he could almost smell the brine from the ocean coming in on the soft breeze. He could almost hear the seals barking a mile away. There were bunches of rosemary and bay leaves in juice glasses on the counter, and he could smell those too. Through the window he could just see the magenta-colored leaves on the liquid amber maples in Bierce Park across the street. "Can I help?" he asked, taking another sip.

"Sure," the prince said at the same time his daughter said "No." The two of them looked at each other and laughed. Isaac laughed, too. Then Lilah brought over some celery to cut. "Fine dice," she ordered, and Isaac didn't even wince.

The prince said, "How was your day, Mr. I?"

"Fine. How was both of yours?" It was satisfying to cut the celery, the crunching sound, the growing pile. He popped a few bits into his mouth and they burst, watery and thready, in his mouth.

Lilah complained about the uselessness of school. Then the prince told a story that he thought was really funny, about how when they were catering there was a nasty woman sending food back to the kitchen, so they all spit in her food. He and Lilah were laughing, and Isaac could have said, That's unsanitary and unethical and unprofessional and you could lose your jobs but instead he just said, "Jeez," and got another beer.

When he asked for seconds of chicken pot pie, he said to Lilah, "You already have your own style of cooking. Comfort food, not 'California umami,' like your mom's."

And Lilah dished him up a big steaming slice and got all enthusiastic. "I'm really into old-school food. You know, hearty, updated, but nutritious, too."

"We're food activists," the prince said.

Isaac told them about how Lilah's mom wouldn't even let him in the kitchen when she was cooking, and then he tried to describe the exact colors of the marijuana in the pipe and then he finished the last of his beer and told them about the *Thriller* party.

"Oh, no," Lilah groaned, at the same time that the prince said, "And we'll cater it."

"I'll pay you!" Isaac said.

"Excellent," the prince said.

Lilah rolled her eyes. "The comeback tour," she said, but she smiled a little.

That very night Isaac went on the web, downloaded some photos of Michael Jackson doing *Thriller* and made an Evite that played the song. He sent it to the whole Manpower email alias. The next day at work he forwarded the email to three of his buddies. Then he sent it to his sister Sadie, who owned a bookstore, apologizing for not answering her calls and texts and emails. Then, he forwarded it to some more random people. His ex, Diane, called to discuss finances and Isaac even invited her, plus the karate teacher. At four p.m. he left work to search for a costume.

During that week preceding the party, Isaac, Lilah and the prince consulted each night at dinner. Isaac purchased a life-sized cut out of Michael Jackson. He couldn't find one from *Thriller*, but this one had on ripped nineties jeans, sneakers and a black leather jacket. Then he printed out color photos of Michael from different periods, except the way he looked right before he died, and taped them around the living room. Each night before he went to bed, Isaac watched YouTube and practiced the *Thriller* dance.

Weirdly, instead of singing *Thriller* all day at work, Isaac kept humming *Rain Drops Keep Fallin' on My Head*, and thinking of that scene in *Butch Cassidy and the Sundance Kid* which he saw when he was a kid, when Paul Newman and Katherine what's-her-name-that-incredibly-hot-actress ride a bike together. Just two friends riding through the countryside, clowning together, sunlight and dandelion fluff and apple eating.

Sometimes Isaac mumble-sang on three descending notes, "'Nothin's worryin' me.'"

Lilah and the prince started prepping for the *Thriller* party around five on Saturday afternoon, right after Lilah painted Isaac's nails electric blue. Lilah told Isaac the appetizers were all 90's inspired, but she kept ordering him out of the kitchen because she wanted it to be a surprise, so Isaac went to take a long bath and get dressed.

"Bam," Isaac said when he popped out of his bedroom an hour later. He had on matching red faux leather pants and jacket. His hair was jelled up into a perfect 80's do, with one greased corkscrew on his forehead.

"Wow," Lilah said.

The prince laughed, but in a nice way.

There was still an hour until the party started. Isaac decided to pour himself an ouzo shot from the fat bottle with the handle he'd purchased for the occasion. Lilah pretended to gag and even the prince winced when he tried it.

By nine Lilah and the prince had the trays ready to go. Isaac relaxed on the couch, sipping ouzo. At nine-thirty no one had arrived. "Fashionably late," Isaac called into the kitchen. Lilah brought out a tasting plate for Isaac. On it, Chinese Chicken Salad with mandarin oranges, pizza bagels, and homemade hot pockets. Plus a Pop Rocks cocktail. Lilah watched while Isaac tasted everything.

At ten p.m. Lilah said, "How many people RSVP'd?"

"Two of my friends wrote that they couldn't come, and one said he'd try. Aunt Sadie's out of town, book buying. I didn't hear from anyone else, but there was no RSVP, anyway," Isaac said.

Lilah looked dangerous. "Why didn't you ask people to RSVP? Why?"

"Let's just see who shows up. I invited this doctor—"

Lilah rolled her eyes. "You know who killed Michael Jackson, right?"

"Did you ever see *Butch Cassidy and The Sundance Kid*?" Isaac asked.

"Sure," the prince said. "The one where the two dudes are totally surrounded but refuse to give up and they die. That's a downer."

Lilah and the prince put the hot pockets and pizza bagels in the oven on warm and the chicken salad and cocktail in the fridge.

At ten-thirty the phone rang. Lilah picked it up.

—"I didn't even know you were invited."

—"Mom, you don't need to make an excuse. No one wanted you or that crap karate teacher to come, anyway." Lilah dropped the phone onto the coffee table and stalked into the kitchen.

Isaac followed her. "Lilah, that wasn't very—" The doorbell rang. Isaac and Lilah stared at each other.

The prince called, "The doctor's here."

Isaac shrugged one shoulder for courage, and walked back into the living room.

The doctor was perched on the arm of the couch holding a Pop Rocks cocktail. The first doctor, Dr. Lucille, the one who replaced Joyce. The allergic twig in a black turtleneck.

"Hi," Isaac said. "You're not in a costume."

The doctor held up her white gloved hand. "This

party's over, am I right? Or did it never get started? Who's more pathetic, you or me, good question, right?"

"Excuse me," Isaac said. He went to the bathroom and stared at himself in the mirror.

"Dad?" Lilah hovered in the door of the bathroom, her face white and pinched and full of worry. "Don't bug out, you don't look so—"

"I was just checking to make sure. I look different, don't I?" Isaac said. "I look cool."

"You do?" Lilah said.

Isaac talked to the Lilah in the mirror. "Sweetie, don't worry so much. I'd almost advise you that it's never too late to change, except that it might make me vomit."

"I'm all about reality," Lilah said.

They heard the volume of the music rise. "They will possess you unless you change that number on your dial." They heard the prince call, "Mr. I, the doctor wants to learn the dance."

Isaac shimmied his head and shoulders. He waved to Lilah with bright electric neon blue nails. "You need to leaven your reality with a little magic, Sweetie. You'll see."

To My
Best Friend
Who Hates
Me

I keep thinking about the things you said when you called, Lucille. I'm not talking about the part where you said ugly shoes. I'm talking about the other parts, where you said that I was a lying whore, and you wish I were dead.

You know very well I'm a no-nonsense, get-back-to-work kind of woman. I mean, hello? I'm a nurse practitioner (I know you've always thought you were better than me because you've got the MD, but it just means you have to work longer hours and pay exorbitant insurance). I signed up for karate in Bierce Park, just to stop your words from taking over my brain. The first day the sensei asked us to stand with our palms facing our chests, our left feet pressed against our right knees, and repeat the mantra, I Am One with All Sentient Beings. Unfortunately, you hijacked my mantra, and all I could hear was: Whore, Wish You Were Dead, Whore, Wish You Were Dead. After a few minutes the headache came, and I had to crouch off to the side with my head in my hands. The sensei, who had one golden eye, said, Your qi is too powerful.

I realize now I have to take more direct action. Think of this as an eviction notice. I will respond to your accusations, calmly and clearly, one by one, and then I will banish all thoughts of you, forever.

1) I'm a whore.
What's with this, Lucille? First of all, what do you have against sex workers? And secondly, in what way am I selling my body for money? I mean, Scott makes less than I do.

2) You wish I were dead.
I don't wish you were dead, because then Scott would feel guilty, and he might blame me, and it would mess up our relationship, but I do wish you would take a long vacation to Nepal or Vancouver, and come back with a new boyfriend, or at least a hobby.

I wish you would stop spitting on me.

(I'm not going to dignify that ugly shoe accusation with its own number, but as you know we are required to wear comfortable shoes for our profession. No one can understand why you wear those giant platform shoes literally made out of rubber tires.)

3) I lie.
It's true, I didn't tell you. But what was I supposed to say? During a break between patients, or after laps in the pool, just, like, Oh, by the way, Lucille, I think your husband is extremely hot. What good would that have done?

I had no idea how quickly fantasies can fill a glance, ease into long looks and jangling nerves.

Still, I decided to put a stop to it. I made an appointment to meet Scott at Bierce Park before work.

We sat in that Once Upon a Time reading bench the bookstore put in facing the basketball court, and we talked about boundaries and responsibility.

We met several more times in the park to talk about limit setting and loyalty, and a few other topics, and then, whether it was bad luck or good luck, someone must have seen us and talked, because you called up and said, Don't play innocent with me, and you said, Ugly shoes, Wish you were dead, etcetera. I don't think I said one word, but I had tunnel vision, and just a couple of months later, Scott left you. And then you left our practice, just never came in again.

There was no time to tell the truth.

4) We swore eternal friendship.
I know you didn't mention that in the phone call, but Scott told me you said that. Yes, we were colleagues, you were a good boss, you're a good doctor, I would never deny that, but I don't remember any bloodletting. No genuflecting, no exchange of tokens or death do us parts.

Okay, I realize you may be thinking about that time when we talked about marrying each other. I remember. We were getting out of the car in front of your house. We could see the lights of the boardwalk, and we could hear the seals. It was a dark night—I remember because you dropped the keys and we were feeling around in the gravel for them. We'd just been to the movies, and we were in one of those moods where everything is funny, like when you're a kid and you drink too much soda. We were hushing each other so we wouldn't wake Scott, sleeping inside. I must have said something like,

Lucille, your hair looks great in a ponytail. Or maybe even, Lucille, you look pretty tonight, which made us laugh again, since it was so dark there was no pretty to be seen.

You told me once that I was the only person in the world who thought you were beautiful. And I really did. I remember at the office party last year you were wearing a red shirt and red lipstick and you were holding your champagne in one hand and a joint in the other. There was something elegant about you. Your eyes were all shiny, and you were talking fast. You were probably mouthing off about John Travolta's double chin, real estate prices, breastfeeding in public. Everything disgusted you. And I remember thinking, Lucille has charisma.

Not like now. Your charisma has inverted, like a black hole. Lately, you look like a thirty-two-year-old Italian widow. You're going to be wearing a kerchief on your head next time I see you. Your veins are filled with spoiled milk. Last week, when you spit on my shoe at the farmer's market, I swear your saliva sizzled when it hit.

Anyway, back to the point. We were on our knees, feeling around for those keys, I had complimented you about one thing or another, and you said, You always make me feel great. I should have married someone like you.

And I said, being practical, But what about sex?

And you said, I can't remember exactly, but something to the effect of it would be a spiritual union.

And I said, I'm not marrying anyone who won't have sex with me. Something like that, and we laughed,

116

and it turned out the keys were under the driver's seat of the car.

Okay. That's it then.

Except, one more thing. You're right, Lucille, I lied to you. I lied to you, okay? And even romance and passion and love can't totally explain the reason why. I've thought a lot about it. How could I betray you?

When I was in tenth grade Advanced Placement Biology, we dissected a fetal calf. The other girls ran gasping from the room, one even fainted, but all I felt was determination. To tell the truth, the smell of formaldehyde electrified me. I couldn't wait to split the skin with the scalpel. That's always the story I've told when I explain why I became an NP, but now I see it's a story about something else, too.

And I remember even before that, when I was a kid, and we played Red Rover in the playground, I would always break through the wall of children holding hands, every time. It didn't matter to me if they sprained their fingers or twisted their wrists and cried. Nothing was going to stop me.

Probably when you played Red Rover you never got through, and then you pitched a fit, and the teacher had to wash your face with a cool cloth in the girl's bathroom. Or maybe you didn't play. Maybe you were too busy giving mouth-to-mouth resuscitation to a dead robin. Or maybe you were one of those girls who sat on the swings all recess, whispering with your best friend.

And now, even though we're not talking, I'm always talking to you in my head. All the time. When I'm in the break room, when I'm typing up medical records, preparing an injection, it's always, And one more thing,

Lucille. And when Scott and I are together, I think, Is this the way he touched Lucille, just like this? And when I touch him, I wonder if I'm tracing the path of your tongue along his body.

I know, weird.

Speaking of weird, I wanted to tell you what happened yesterday. I was examining a new patient, and I noticed she had an indentation in her lower back. The indentation looked like an empty bowl. I asked her about it. She told me it was the place where a surgeon had excised her fetal twin. In utero, this woman had absorbed her twin into her own body, and there it lay, curled inside her all those years. When they discovered the twin through an X-ray, the woman didn't blanch. She simply said, Get rid of it. The woman said that after the surgery she felt great, like she'd lost ten pounds.

Now I've lost track of the number I was on. Where was I?

There Once Was A Woman Who Longed for A Child

This woman owned a used bookstore called Bierce Park Books, her life's passion, though there had also been a brief, great love, a Chilean researcher who left the country and never returned, and then she rebounded with the old professor, who had already chewed up and spit out an entire family of his own. By the time the courtship was over and they were ready to begin on a baby, the bookstore owner's hair was turning prematurely grey and the professor was emeritus.

It was then that the woman began to desire a child. With the professor's low sperm count and her irregular periods, the doctor was not optimistic, but still the woman stretched mucus between thumb and forefinger, drew blue bridges between the dots on her temperature chart; whenever the blue line spiked, they began babymaking with a vengeance. With each thrust, the woman thought, I wish.

There once was a woman who longed for a child, but month after lumpen month passed with nothing to show. The woman tried raising her knees after ejaculation, curled around her uterus, lulling the egg into submission. Next, she went to a Chinese herbalist.

He prescribed large, green, hay-tasting pills. Nothing. Then, Clomid, white, tasteless pills. On top of the Clomid, artificial insemination, the old professor jerking off to French *Vogue* in a cubicle. By this time, a diaper commercial on television could make the woman weep. Finally, she took the money left from her grandfather Albert's inheritance and invested all of it in IVF (the old professor felt they should now bow to fate and would contribute no money and only a grudging amount of sperm). The woman agreed she would try only once. He would not inject her in the ass every morning. She asked her brother Isaac to do it, but he sent his doctor friend Lucille instead. The woman would watch her own face in the medicine cabinet mirror as Lucille slid the needle in, and she would think of Ahab and his whale.

There once was a woman who longed for a child. And she was thrice blessed, triplets. The physician urged selective reduction, the suctioning of one fetus so the others might prosper. The old professor said, One is an elegant sufficiency, two is one too many.

But it was always the youngest of three in the fairy tales, the third who made the difference, the unbalancer, the unhinger, the unexpected. Beyond that, the woman felt that three was a given, the element in her story that could not be altered. Despite the old professor and Isaac and Lucille's pleas for reason, she kept them all.

Then, the nausea took over, and for three months she thought of nothing but what she might be able to keep down: white bread rolled into pills and swallowed, sometimes a cracker, and magically, frozen chicken pot pies. Next, she grew monstrous, her muscles separating in a dark stripe down her stomach. She could hardly walk, it burned so between her legs, as if she had to pee or come, but neither urination nor masturbation relieved it. She would not have been surprised to see a small hand or foot slipping out between her legs.

In the sonograms the technician assured her that each child floated alone, separated one from the other by a thin membrane. The woman studied the image of the three inside her, but she could not make out the walls. Her children seemed pressed together, belly to back, hand to hand, inseparable. Then, in the sixth month, her cervix began to open, and they sewed her shut with transparent thread. She lay on her back for the last months, increasing, waiting.

Once there was a woman who longed for a child. Thirty-fourth week, cervix untied, in early labor, the monitor indicates fetal distress. Emergency c-section. In the crescendo of birth, her masked husband's tired hand on her forehead, her brother Isaac holding her hand, the anesthesiologist hooked a small white curtain across her neck so she would not see her stomach rupture. Numbed from the waist down, she felt a tug, but no pain. A tiny, perfectly formed child floated from behind the magic curtain. Isaac and the new girl began to cry. As the second miniature girl pulled free, already pink and yelling, the woman felt her own ascension. And then the gloved hands untethered the boy, a blue creature, a changeling child who, for his own reasons, preferred not to breathe.

The woman could not exaggerate the importance of that moment, when all boundaries had been overrun. This was her story's crisis. She had given everything she had, and it was only the beginning.

There Once Was A Man Who Longed for A Child

After his wife left him for the karate teacher, the man raised his daughter up until the September she left for cooking school. That October, the man sorted through all the things his daughter had bagged to throw out, and kept most of it, and sent her three care packages. In November, he truly began to live alone.

November: the most beautiful month of the year in central California, beautiful because of the cool weather and the slanted light and the magenta-colored leaves on the liquid amber maples in Bierce Park across from the man's apartment. The man used to take his daughter to karate lessons in the park, but now, through his window, he watched the retirees practice tai chi in rough synchronicity, and the homeless people debate the park ranger, and the dogs collegially sniff each other's butts. He watched for hours. Sometimes he became mesmerized by the gold-to-wine-colored leaves on the trees, their gentle breathing.

On weekdays, when he unlocked the door after work, the evening stretched out, all his. For dinner he ate what he wanted, sometimes a rotisserie chicken from the grocery store, sometimes a three-egg omelet with ketchup.

After dinner the man drank Dragon's Breath IPA and binge-watched *Friday Night Lights*. In the season one finale, we find out that the football coach and his hot wife have made a mistake, getting pregnant when their daughter is already grown, and then in the second season they end up with a gremlin-faced baby named Gracie Belle sporting a yellow mullet. The man wondered why they had chosen an infant so lacking in star appeal, but oddly it was around then that he began to long for a baby of his own—the chubby legs pincering his waist, the milk-sour smell of its head. And all the cute things they said when they began to talk. Accompanied by his beer, he now found himself watching YouTube videos of babies saying the darndest things. His favorite was a two-year-old trying to unbuckle her seat belt. Her father asked if she needed help, and the two-year-old yelled, Worry about yourself! Worry about yourself!

Finally, the man thought he might be getting malnourished from lack of vegetables, so the next Sunday he forced himself to go to the farmer's market. He wandered the stalls, pondering over the largest tomato or zucchini or apple, then dropping them in his backpack. He came upon the last stall selling gourds and dried flowers and branches and dried grasses all ablaze in fall colors. On the far left of the front table, on a blue dish towel decorated with red foxes lay a pile of shriveled roots. One was curved like a C. The top part of the root had two protrusions, almost like bulging eyes. And it actually had a green tendril, maybe a half inch long, growing up from its head.

The proprietor was busy helping a customer choose between a bouquet of glittering dried corn and a bouquet of cattails, but a teenaged girl with an afro like a halo sat on a folding chair behind the back table, reading from a tablet.

The man said, Do you know what these roots are?

Barleycorn, said the girl, not glancing up. For chickens.

I don't think these are barleycorns, the man said. They're some kind of root or tuber. This one is sprouting.

The girl shrugged. I just work here.

The man looked over to the owner of the stall for assistance, but the customer had begun to cry.
How much are they?

The girl did not look up. Three dollars each.

That's crazy, the man laughed. The owner was now embracing the weeping customer, so the man paid the high price, and secured the root in the front zippered pocket of his backpack.

Back home, he took a pot with a dead cactus out of his daughter's room. He pulled out the cactus with an oven mitt to avoid the prickers, then buried the root just up to its eyes in the dry dirt. He watered it under the faucet. Then he put it on the windowsill above the sink. Why not?

When he got home from work on Monday the little stem was at least a half inch taller, and there was a tiny furled leaf coming out of it. Down below and between the bulging eyes there was another lump—it looked almost like the top of a wide nose.

By the next weekend, a second tendril was curling out of its head, the first tiny leaf had opened, and a whole face had emerged, just the chin left in the dirt. A pug nose with no nostrils, but still.

It could not be denied that his so-called barleycorn was thriving. Only two weeks and its chin was out of the dirt, raised a little, the beige, freckled head tilted over to the right, almost as if it were resting its cheek on the ground. Three small new heart-shaped leaves had sprouted out of its head. He was sure, almost sure, he imagined telling his daughter Lilah.

The weeks went by and the barleycorn continued to emerge from the dirt, until one day the man noticed its head was filthy. He got a washcloth from the bathroom, wrung it out, and carefully began to clean the little face. When the warm cloth was over the barleycorn's nose, it sneezed.

"Did you hear that?" the man said out loud.

The man pulled the cloth off. He was almost sure he had heard a tiny, brilliant sneeze. Nothing now, no movement. The man had an idea. He warmed some milk on the stove, dipped his pinky to make sure it was right. He dripped some into the soil.

The next morning his barleycorn had grown arms. Dirty, rootlet-covered, lumpy little arms like two carrots except beige, reaching out of the dirt, reaching up like, Hold me. Like, More milk, please. The man couldn't stop smiling as he warmed milk for both himself and the barleycorn. He stood by the sink and they both 'drank' from the same mug.

A few mornings later, the man woke to remember that in the middle of the night he had heard mewling. He had stumbled out of bed, shuffled into the hall. A thin cry, like a kitten, from downstairs. In the moonlight over the sink, the barleycorn's mouth was a little sienna-colored O, its potato eyes still closed, crying in its sleep. The man warmed milk, dripped it into the now open mouth. He whisper-sang to it, *Bye Baby Bunting, Papa's gone a hunting, to fetch a little rabbit skin*… The crying trailed off. Then it began to coo. The man leaned over the sink, his neck pressed against the cool faucet, and put his ear up to the pursed potato mouth. It was making those strange newborn baby sounds, little grunts and snuffles. The man felt moist, milky breath on his ear.

And then the very next day, his daughter came home for break, brandishing a new tattoo on the side of her foot: I am corn. This seemed like a startling coincidence, but his daughter explained that it was an ironic comment on the overuse of corn products by GMOs. That night, after his daughter had dumped her clothes out of the suitcase onto the floor, she jumped on the couch and beckoned him in. As they cuddled together, his daughter scoffed at *Friday Night Lights*, and said they should watch a documentary on foie gras and the ethics of force feeding. The following day while the daughter lay on the couch reading a book called *The Wild Table*, the man did her laundry. The daughter called him over to show him all the edible things they could forage for, right in the park across the street.

The man said, his heart quickening, I want to show you my plant. The daughter wouldn't get up, so the father brought it over and put it on the coffee table.

Cute, the daughter said.

Do you think it looks like anything?

His daughter took another look, and said, Yeah, totally, and she pulled out her phone and showed her father a tree in which all the pears looked like laughing buddhas, and a fleeceflower that seemed to a tuber shaped exactly like a grown woman, its roots like long hair.

The barleycorn began to snuffle in its sleep then, and the man said to his daughter, But, can you hear that?

Whoa, his daughter said, and played her father a translation of plants talking through transducers and amplifiers. It sounded like a robot purring. Then she played him the noise coming from the Rosetta comet, which sounded like a squirrel chattering.

That night the daughter cooked her father his favorite dinner, meat lasagna with béchamel sauce, and poured them both a glass of wine, but during dinner the fussing of the barleycorn made it hard to concentrate on his daughter's discussion about whether she should take Sustainability Two or Cuisines and Cultures of Africa. Are you listening? the daughter asked. The man doused the plant with milk and set it on the little table by the front door.

After dinner his daughter went out with her friends to dumpster dive. The man dozed. Though he thought he heard crying in his sleep, he didn't wake fully. The anxious dozing felt deeply familiar. At three a.m. he heard a crash downstairs and a scream and then laughter and whispering. His daughter was probably drunk, but now that she was home the man could finally sleep deeply.

When he came downstairs the next morning there was a boy sprawled on the couch and a girl in the fetal position on the loveseat. In the entryway, a smear of dirt on the floor. The terracotta pot had been cracked in half and set back onto the little table next to the barleycorn, half-flattened by a shoe.

And even while the man carried the barleycorn out to the compost bucket and gently laid it over the leftovers from last night's dinner, he noticed his sadness was oddly mixed with relief. As he put the green ventilated lid back on the bucket, he thought that maybe it was best that the cries of plants were generally not audible to human ears.

On the day before his daughter left to go back to cooking school, the man walked with her in the park across the street. The daughter remembered that she used to take karate there.

When I went through my blocks you would do them with me, like little ghost blocks off to the side, she said.

I remember, the man answered.

They wandered the rows of now mostly bare maples, and the man wondered what would happen on season three of *Friday Night Lights*. His daughter squeezed his hand and said, I'm applying for a cooking internship in Ghana for the summer. Maybe you can visit me there. All the while the man kept hearing shuffling in the leaves off to the right, but he assumed it was a dog nosing the ground or perhaps a homeless person turning in his sleeping bag. He didn't see the squat figure dressed in a jerkin of lasagna noodles, with bulgy eyes and a wide, freckled nose, with a bald, half-smashed-in head and stubby, tuberous legs with no feet. The one that whispered, or did not whisper, More milk, please.

Lost In Père Lachaise Cemetery

I looked up at the imposing stone entryway guarded by hourglasses on each side. Fitting, since it was here that I planned to reunite with my former lover after fifteen years. And there he was amidst the crowd, now bald, with a grizzled salt-and-pepper beard and sporting an unfortunate loud blue polo shirt with green stripes.

He had wandered into my bookstore fifteen years before, and we fell instantly in love. A visiting Chilean researcher at the university, when his visa expired he returned to Chile. We sent torrid emails to each other for several months, and then, just like that, I received a formal and apologetic message: the obstacles too many, best to end communication now, always love you, blah, blah, blah. Crack went my heart.

Now, fifteen years later at the entrance to the famous Parisian cemetery, I was almost upon him when he finally saw me. He stood, he smiled, those eyes, and it was just like before, like the night Obama won, and we all found ourselves rushing into the streets. Or, like a door to a magical world in a children's book. Like the snarl I thought permanently lodged in my chest had suddenly untangled.

He went in for the traditional Latin American kiss

on the cheek, I was confused, our lips touched. Up close I saw that he had one silver earring in his ear, which could have looked outdated and sad on a middle-aged man, but with the bald head and the beard, actually looked jaunty and piratical, if you ignored the shirt.

We entered the cemetery together. It was magical, dappled with green light, tree-lined and mossy. The winding paths were marked with miniature street signs, and the multitudes of stone family crypts with their pointy roofs at rakish angles looked like an abandoned child-sized city. Our shoulders and hands bumped and brushed.

But if I've learned anything over the years, it's that things are never that easy. For example, the reason it took so long for him to see me? He was arguing with his fourteen-year-old son. This boy was already as tall as his father, but skinny, with his father's former messy dark hair, shoulders up around his ears, a look of outrage on his face. He greeted me with a shrug, then pulled his father ahead as we walked and began yelling at him in Spanish.

Also cropped out of the original romantic picture: my twin nine-year-old daughters, close behind me, and my husband, back in the U.S. While I walked with my ex-lover the girls had crowded round, stepping on my heels, and when they saw the tumultuous scene between father and son, they grabbed onto my arm and shirt, began whispering furiously, one daughter the lead, the other the chorus.

What are they saying? Why are they fighting? I'm hot. Me, too. I'm hungry. So am I. Your friend is weird and so is his son. Yeah. Why are we at a cemetery? I hate it here. I do, too. We want to leave. Can we just leave?

I answered as soothingly as I could. "I don't know why they are fighting, but he is not weird, he is a very old and important friend of mine. This is the most famous, beautiful cemetery in the world."

My daughter Sarah, who we call Little My after the feisty character in the Moomintroll books, and who at nine, and to her great consternation and perhaps due to her lifelong love affair with milk and the attendant onslaught of growth hormones, already had her period and looked like a miniature Marilyn Monroe, flipped her platinum blond hair and cried, "Why are we always doing what you want to do? I want to climb the Eiffel Tower and eat a snail."

"But couldn't this also be fun?" I asked. "You could learn Spanish. Couldn't it be an adventure?"

"I hate adventures," cried my other daughter, the chorus, the one we call Mymble, Little My's dreamier sister in the books, my little lactose intolerant mouse with brown hair and round brown eyes.

During a pause in the son's yelling, my once-and-perhaps-future lover stopped walking and turned around, smiling apologetically. Awash in the hallucinatory heat of Paris in midsummer, all three children sank onto the stone curb, their first communal act, although probably a coincidence. Already worn down myself, I thought to say, Why don't we just try to meet later? After the girls and I go to the Eiffel Tower and eat a snail.

But my former lover bounced on his toes, as I suddenly remembered he was inclined to do, "I have a game! You have one hour to find three graves—Heloise and Abelard, Oscar Wilde and Maria Callas." Then he repeated himself in Spanish for the benefit of his son.

All three stared up at him, but I was infected by his enthusiasm, as always.

"Wait," I said, suddenly realizing we had no points of reference, no cell phones, no GPS. "I'll go back and buy a map. Then we can all search for the graves together. Wait here!" I called as I ran back down the short hill to the entrance.

In May, after fifteen years of silence, I had suddenly received an email with the subject 'from Daniel,' and inside, just one sentence: "Sadie, are you happy?" That question first infuriated and then plagued and disturbed me for weeks. I drafted a long email defensively describing my charming daughters, the expansion of the bookstore, even my husband's publication record and collection of classic noir DVDs, but finally I simply wrote back: "Why did you disappear?" He answered with a photo of his son. He wrote that two months after his return to Chile he had slept with an old girlfriend. She got pregnant and decided to keep the baby. He didn't know how to tell me he had cheated on me, much less that he was becoming a father and would have to stay in Chile to co-parent, though he hastened to add in the email that he and the woman never lived together, and she was now married to a very nice man. My lover had become the director of a nonprofit called Peace in Our Time, and would be at a conference in Paris in the beginning of August. Would I join him? I could use his cousin's Airbnb apartment for free, while he and his son stayed at the conference hotel.

"I'm so sorry. I made a terrible mistake. I was not young enough to have been so stupid. Nations mean nothing. Home is where the heart sits inside, isn't that the saying? Still and always you are the woman of my life. With sweet honesty," he ended his email.

In the daily messages that followed, my former lover outlined his vague but hopeful plans for our future: maybe we could help the mother of his child, who played third violin for the Orquestra Filarmonica de Santiago, find a job in the Bay Area. As well as her husband, who played the double bass. Or, perhaps with the current state of affairs in Gringolandia better to try our luck in a new locale? Maybe he could keep his Director of Development job in Chile and telecommute, and I could put my bookstore online. Iceland? Or we could start our own nonprofit in Southeast Asia. Or a bilingual catering business in Berlin, the three children dressed in black and white, serving locally grown South American inspired hors d'oeuvres and organic champagne on silver trays.

"Ah, I see you have returned to your Sturm und Drang mode. Last time you nearly killed yourself and certainly damaged your health with the fertility treatments and the ill-advised pregnancy and subsequent postpartum depression with the result that now in my dotage I am blessed with twin tweens. I thought you were exhausted with your store and your political activities and the girls, but now I see it was just an intermission while you gathered your forces. I hope you'll forgive me if I just sit on the sidelines this time around." That's what my perfectly decent husband said when I broke the news

134

that I was taking the girls and going to Paris to meet my ex-lover. He then returned to his book. This might sound horribly dismissive, but it was in fact a generous invitation—our best times together had always been reading side by side. He was an emeritus professor, and we had been partners for more than a decade, with separate bank accounts, a chore wheel, and a sex date every second Thursday right after Stephen Colbert.

My mother fired questions at me over the phone: "What about the bookstore? Have you thought of the cost of this little adventure? For everyone involved? Let Angelina Jolie and Brad Pitt be a warning to you." When I went over to tell my brother Isaac, a single dad with a horticulture obsession, he whispered because his plants didn't like loud noises, "Are we talking about that same bastard who broke your heart a million years ago?" Then he read a text from his friend Lucille aloud: "Green card. Green card anyone?" His daughter Lilah, just home from college, called from the kitchen, "Go for it. Your husband's an old mansplainer."

Mostly I thought of my grandfather, Albert. A widower in a retirement community in Florida, he had suddenly fallen in love with a man and spent the last ten years of his life with him. I remember Grandpa Albert telling me, "Anytime anyone takes a risk everyone always says it won't work. That's what they said about the American revolution. That's what they said about me and Buster, too."

There was a line of ten people to buy a map. The old vendor was having a difficult conversation with someone who didn't speak French, so they were trying to understand each other in the few words of English they shared while everyone else sighed and tapped their feet or tried to help translate. Someone behind me said, "I have a map."

I turned. Up against the gate, half-hidden under a leafy tree, an international hippie type with an accordion around his neck had spread his wares out on a burlap cloth. He was wearing a green t-shirt and green ripped cargo pants, with several strings of beads, amulets and bags jostling around his neck, green feathered earrings in both ears, dreaded, sandy-colored hair, an upturned nose. His eyes were so green I assumed he was wearing tinted contacts. He was selling various small, clay, potbellied figures, some solitary, some entwined in vaguely sexual positions. They were all faceless. I thought they might be fertility goddesses or maybe fetishes. If I hadn't been in a rush to get back I would have asked him if he'd made the little figures or if they were imported and from where. He was smiling as if he'd just thought of something very amusing, or as if he were high. The map he held out to me was rolled into a tube with twine knotted around it. He said, "Five euros. The initial cost is very low. It's the unofficial version, full of mischief, for those who like to take risks." From his accent, I thought he might be Irish. "It has funny stories about the people buried here." When I smiled hesitantly, he said, "Your little girls will love it."

"How do you know I have children?" That seemed stalkerish, but then I thought perhaps he had seen us as we entered.

"One euro," he said, gesturing with the map towards the line that had not moved.

I bought it.

As I walked back, I unrolled the map, which seemed to be made of parchment. It had been very carefully hand-drawn in green ink. Along the border was a list of all the famous people buried in Pere Lachaise with a number that corresponded to a numbered grave on the map. Some of the monuments had cartoon bubbles coming out of them, with little stories about the departed. I scanned down the list of graves. Clearly, every great romantic had decided to spend eternity in Pere Lachaise. Colette, Sarah Bernhardt, Edith Piaf, Isadora Duncan and of course Heloise and Abelard. All of these people who had shown courage in love. I felt a quickening of renewed hope.

Before I turned right onto the smaller avenue, I heard my lover whistling a cheerful, complicated tune, drawing me near. When I turned the corner, there he was, all by himself. My first thought was something like, Alone at last, quickly followed by a shock of guilt and fear. "Where are the kids?" I asked.

"They've gone off to encounter the graves."

I said, "Was your son with the twins by any chance?"

"They just rushed off here and there, I'm not sure who was with who, all mixed up maybe!" He laughed, like, how wonderful, how absurd!

"How will they know when an hour is up?" I inquired as calmly as I could. "They don't have watches. They are nine years old. They can't even ask how to get back here because they don't know where here is, and anyway, they don't speak French."

"Neither does anyone else—everyone here is either dead or a tourist, mi amor."

I looked at him, his jolly, open face, his silver pirate hoop. I wondered if perhaps he had always been piratical in a reckless, let's all just walk the plank kind of way.

"Mi amor, no te preocupes, we'll find them," my lover said, finally noticing my distress.

"How?" I asked quietly.

"We'll go to each of the graves I told them to find, and we'll gather them up! Like Gringo Easter egg hunts! En todo caso, I am sure my son is supervising them. He is very responsible."

"We can use this map," I said, guilty that I had one, while I had left my children without. I felt my lover's warm breath on the back of my neck as he looked over my shoulder at the map. There was this little tug-of-war in my heart, lust-love on one side, guilt-anxiety-love on the other, and I wondered if that was just what it felt like to be in a blended family. I said, trying to be humorous, "If this were fiction, we would definitely be doomed. Adulterers always fare badly in literature, and stepmothers fare worse."

My lover replied cheerfully, "But is it really adultery if you're reuniting with your true love? And why do you think fairytales are always about stepmothers? Nuclear families are bound by genetics, but stepfamilies are full of infinite possibility!"

I thought of my girls asking for help with their American accents, and hoped they would be pitied rather than despised. I felt a familiar knot gathering again in my chest, and I wondered if the spell he had put on me might already be wearing off.

Meanwhile, in another part of the graveyard, so I

learned later, my daughters were indeed wandering, lost and alone, except for each other. They didn't look at any of the names on any of the gravestones, and they didn't look at the dark mouths of the crypts. They didn't leave breadcrumbs in their wake.

"I don't like dead people," Mymble said.

"I prefer the undead," Little My said.

"Good point," Mymble said.

They continued on in silence. Then Mymble grabbed her sister's wrist. "Listen," she whispered. "Someone's following us."

At about the same time my lover's fourteen-year-old son was kicking up pebbles and giving dirty looks to the other tourists. Up ahead on the right he noticed a graffitied grave littered with tokens. A dreadlocked hippie with an accordion around his neck sat on a marble slab a few graves down, swinging his legs. My lover's son was curious about the guy—but he was also shy, so he pretended to be interested in the messy grave. It belonged to James Douglas Morrison, 1943-1971. Whoever that is, he thought.

The hippie called over to him, "Me das fuego?"

The boy shook his head.

"Me pasas el encendidor." The boy reached into the litter in front of the grave and fished out a lighter. When he walked up to him, the hippie continued in Spanish, "There are things known and things unknown and in between are the doors." He lifted his chin towards the grave. "He said that." The hippie scooted his butt farther back onto the grave and leaned against the headstone. He pulled a hand-made cigarette out of one of the pouches on his neck and ran it along his upper lip. My lover's son flicked the lighter. It worked.

The hippie took a drag. The green smoke that billowed out of his mouth smelled like strawberries. He gestured with a tilt of his head for the boy to sit next to him, which he did.

"So what else did the guy say?" asked the boy.

"You know what it says on his grave in Latin? Be true to your own spirit, or maybe demon, depends what you think daemon means." The hippie uncinched a little rainbow colored woven pouch around his neck and carefully shook out a shriveled brown vegetable onto his palm. He held it out to my lover's son.

"What is it?" the boy asked.

"It will unchain you, release your true spirit, if you're willing to take a chance. It's a hundred percent organic. I harvested it myself."

"Over there!" Mymble whispered. "Someone's hiding behind that house for dead people. Didn't you hear it?"

"Okay, I heard it. Shut up."

"Let's run," Mymble whimpered.

"Not an option. I'm going to kick some pervert ass." Fear made Little My furious and bold, as did many other things.

"No, don't! Stay here," Mymble pleaded, pinching the hem of her sister's shirt.

"Don't be a baby." Little My twisted out of her grip. "I'll be right back."

Heloise and Abelard rested side by side, two white statues laid out on white stone coffins. Their marble home was under construction, however, with scaffolding and dirty plastic draped over it.

The children were, of course, not there. The knot in my chest began to feel like a thorn bush. I tried not to think of kidnappers, terrorists, tried to remember that finding the graves was our best chance of finding our children.

"It's nice," my lover said, a catch in his voice. He took my hand. I remembered then that my lover is a perfect hand holder. He has a surprisingly smallish, gentle hand that is never sweaty, and he knows just how to weave his fingers loosely with mine, without squeezing too tightly or dropping it. The opposite of Heloise and Abelard's, whose hard marble hands were pressed against themselves in prayer. Were they praying to be together? Or, were they thanking God for being reunited at last?

I knew he felt that our love was like Abelard and Heloise's. Undying, connected body and soul, except not doomed in the same way. Which reminded me to read what the map had to say on the subject. I unlaced my fingers from his to read.

It said, "Though tragically separated, the lovers corresponded for over 20 years, eternally one. Or is there another story?"

"Aha!" I said, and read aloud to my lover that, in fact, Abelard had been Heloise's tutor. He got her pregnant, married her in secret so it wouldn't spoil his reputation, and was then castrated by her irate family. He finally told her in a letter that he had never loved her but only lusted after her. "That's the greatest love story of all time?" I asked him. I felt a kind of triumphal bitterness in reading the second part to him. I think I actually wanted to see his smile wilt, but he just laughed. "Who knows what's really true," he said, infuriatingly.

Meanwhile, Mymble sat abandoned upon a black slab of marble crying quietly so as not to draw attention to herself. She heard music. The music came closer. She lifted her tear-stained face to a young man dressed all in green playing an accordion.

"Would you like some strawberries?" he asked.

"I'm not allowed to talk to strangers," she said.

"Your mother talked to a stranger, and he turned out to be her prince charming. Don't you want to throw caution to the wind like your mother did?"

She considered, tilted her head to study his face, wiped her nose with her shirt.

"Aren't you tired of being called a baby?" he asked.

She pulled up the strap on one of her daisy-covered sandals. She nodded.

We consulted the map. I traced a path to Wilde's grave with my finger. We headed out, through warrens of paths and clots of tourists. I heard German, Portuguese and maybe Russian. I wanted to ask all of them if they'd seen my children, but it seemed an absurd question, especially in English. "Isn't this wonderful," my lover asked. I kept my eye out for sinister types.

We climbed the hill, up and up, took some turns and arrived at Oscar Wilde's grave.

The map read, "Oscar Wilde, who wrote, 'The advantage of the emotions is that they lead us astray.'" The map went on to report that the art deco angel on top of Oscar Wilde's monument had originally sported an enormous phallus, but it had been broken off and carried away.

Admirers had left many lipsticked kisses all over the angel. There were also offerings, a gold cigarette case, a marble, a disposable razor, and a clay figurine I recognized. I leaned down and picked up the little potbellied manikins embracing. There was a lock of Little My's platinum blond hair wrapped round and round the neck of one of the figures.

"We need to contact the gendarmes," I said.

The breeze on my lover's son's face felt almost unbearably sweet, as did the velvet of his own skin and the smoothness of the marble and stone he trailed his hands along. In fact, the whole world had softened, but at the same time, the colors had brightened. It was a new world, like Avatar in 3-D. He noticed then that everything was pulsing gently—the walkway, the bushes. Even the graves were rising and falling as the dead people breathed underneath. In fact, this tree up ahead, he could see it breathing, too. He ran his hand along its smooth grey bark, kissed one of its leaves. He realized he was connected to the tree by his own primordial past, when he was a monkey boy. He began to swing up into the tree. It was easy, now that he had discovered his inner chimpanzee.

Once he was hidden in the leaves, high up in his leaf nest, higher than he would have ever felt comfortable climbing before, his monkey feet and hands gripping the branches, he peered down at the cemetery. He felt this great tenderness for all things, all the living and the dead. He could feel invisible tendrils of light connecting him with his father and his mother and his stepfather and even with that annoying gringa who was supposedly his father's long lost love and her so-called twins that didn't even look alike or even like they were the same age. He thought about his father's work, Peace in Our Time, and he saw that it really was possible, if you could just wake everyone to the truth. It was so simple. People were like these leaves, not noticing they were all connected to the same tree. He reached out his arms so he could touch all the leaves. He felt his curly monkey feet sliding off the limb, and the leaves sliding out of his fingers. It was okay. He knew someone would catch him.

When Little My stomped around the far side of the crypt she saw a little band of very handsome men in coats and tails and top hats gathered around a large monument. The whole upper half of the stone rectangle was taken up with the wings and body of an angel warrior, chest forward, carved all in right angles. Little My felt a yearning connection to that fierce angel at once.

The men were having a little soiree. They each held a large sunflower and a glass of golden champagne, and they were painting each other's lips a violent plum color. They took turns laying a sunflower on the grave and then ceremoniously kissing the stone. One man's top hat fell off when he bent to pucker, and they found this very funny. After each kiss they would say "Huzzah!" and toast. They were creating a lovely purple bouquet of kisses.

The man who was in the act of kissing the grave turned suddenly. He stared right at her. His face was very vivid, his lips so purple, his eyes a brilliant green. His swallow-tailed coat and top hat were also green. He smiled a little amused smile and beckoned to her with two fingers.

Little My emerged. The men gathered around her. The green-eyed man carefully painted a swirly purple moustache on Little My. Everyone applauded. Then he pulled off his green top hat. A mess of ropey dreads fell around his face. He gently fit the hat on my daughter's head and carefully stuffed all her long blond hair inside. Then he took off his coat, and my daughter put it on.

When my daughter leaned in to kiss Oscar Wilde's grave, she didn't know what made her do it, but she pressed her lips between the angel's legs, right on the part that was missing. Everyone applauded.

"You think an Irish accordion playing hippie kidnapped all three children?" my lover said to me.

"Maybe just Little My."

"I'm sure they're all waiting for us at Maria Callas' memorial. I have always wanted to pay homage there."

I read from the map, skipping the part about how she opened a new door for all the singers of the world. "Maria Callas, who gave up her career for Aristotle Onassis. After Onassis left her for Jackie Kennedy, she died of a heart attack, alone in Paris."

My lover countered, "Maria Callas' upper register was light as an oboe, and her lower register dark and thick like molasses. Her voice was so full of emotion, so beautiful, it was almost ugly."

"It says here that Maria Callas' ashes were stolen from the cemetery, recovered and thrown in the Aegean Sea—her grave is empty!" I said.

"It's not empty—it is filled with the love of all who have visited her here."

"I don't remember you ever talking about Marie Callas. When did you start loving Maria Callas?" I asked.

"Everyone loves Maria Callas."

"Do you love her more than you love your son?"

"What?"

"You heard me."

"Sadie, I don't understand. We're all here in the same place. It's like wandering about a museum. We'll meet up. Everyone is enjoying themselves, I'm sure of it. Are you having some kind of episode?"

"This is what I'm like now," and as I said it, I realized it was true. "I've changed. You left me, then I married a man I wasn't in love with, there was the in vitro, everyone said just to carry one to term, but I insisted on three, one of my babies died, and Mymble almost died, too, she was born so small." I took a shuddery breath. "And now for the last year we've all been wearing these ridiculous pink hats and writing our senators and arguing amongst ourselves while 'he who shall not be named' turns us into—into something ugly," I said, suddenly too exhausted to find the right metaphor.

"I'm so sorry about your child. I wish I had been there." There seemed to be tears in his eyes.

I felt tears threaten my own eyes. "I try to stay hopeful, but all the hope's been beaten out of me. Really, I'm always waiting for the other shoe to drop."

"You also fear shoes?"

"No. Listen, I don't believe there will be peace in our time. Your job is a waste of time. I believe in entropy."

"But then why are you taking this wild chance with me?"

146

Am I taking this chance with you, I thought. Why am I here? Temporary insanity? My last gasp? "Love?"

"So, you do have hope. You do believe in happily ever after after all?"

I had already told him I believed in entropy plus we were surrounded by dead people. "No."

We looked at each other. "Mi amor, Maria Callas was given a great gift and then had to struggle to live with it. We also were given a gift, the gift of love. After all these years, will you struggle with me even if you believe perfect happiness is impossible?"

I didn't answer.

"Could you perhaps struggle for a glorious failure?" He held his hand out.

"Okay." I took his hand. I laughed, but I was crying, too. "So, you still want to be with me, even though I'm a bitter, married woman from a shithole country?"

"Without question." He smiled his enormous smile.

I looked at him searchingly.

"What?" he asked.

"I just thought, maybe you were going to reveal something, too, some way you've changed over the years, some hidden weakness."

He looked puzzled. "This is me, mi amor." He pinched his wide nose.

So, he had no idea what his weakness was, that was certainly somewhat unbearable, in fact that was his weakness.

We kissed.

"I can't go find Maria Callas," I said.

"Esta bien, mi amor."

"I have to find my daughters."

"Esta bien. You go find the children, mi amor. I will find Maria Callas, and we will meet." My lover looked at me with pity and love, and said, "Go, go. I'll meet you there."

"Where?" I asked.

He laughed loud, like he couldn't believe how witty I was. Then he walked into the maze of crypts.

I started downhill. As soon as I was away from his spell of optimism my worry tightened into full-on chest pains. When I turned onto the main broad avenue, I began to run, on the lookout for gendarmes with automatic weapons.

That's when I saw a man fall out of a tree. He landed with a dusty thud. When I approached, I saw that it was not a man, but my lover's son, curled in the fetal position.

"My God! Are you all right?" I said.

He groaned.

I picked him up like a giant baby and dusted him off. He was scraped and bruised. Leaves fell out of his fists when he opened them. I patted him down. Nothing seemed to be broken. He embraced me. His tears and snot wet my neck.

"I knew you will catch me," he said in English.

"What were you doing in that tree?" I asked.

"Working for world peace," he answered.

I looked at the map to re-orient myself. That's when I noticed something I hadn't seen before. There was a golden star painted on top of a building, with Maria Callas' name next to it, and hanging from the final swirly S was a sandal. I held the map closer. A tiny meticulously drawn daisy-covered sandal.

"We have to find Maria Callas' grave," I told my lover's son. He took my hand with his moist and dirty one. I glanced at him. His pupils were strangely huge. Following the map, I led him uphill and to the right until we found ourselves inside an enormous white building with many hallways, all lined from floor to ceiling with thousands of little metal memorial plaques. How would we possibly find Maria Callas amongst them all?

That's when we heard the antique, wheezing sound of accordion music. My lover's son careened toward the sound.

Trying to keep up, I yanked open a heavy wooden door and entered a new hallway. There at the other end, just where it turned a corner, under the golden letters of Maria Callas' name, bobbed the green man, right hand playing the accordion keys, the left pressing silver buttons at the same time, the folds in between expanding and contracting, the music low and slow, then silent, then quick and high. He smiled at me.

Mymble rode his shoulders.

"Mommy," she said. Her face and shirt were covered in blood.

I felt this power rising up from my clotted center. I raised my arm and pointed at the man. I could feel my voice rolling up my throat. I think if the words had come out, they would have been something like Get Gone. A thunderous exorcism. A tremendous relief. Who knows, maybe peace in our time.

But then my lover danced around the far corner, whistling along. He took one of Mymble's hands. Next, Little My appeared in a top hat, graffitied in purple lipstick, dancing a kind of solitary tango. And my lover's son, doing a pathetic version of the moonwalk. Mymble waved at me with her free hand, and the blood on her face and shirt turned to strawberry stains. They all saw me, then, and smiled and welcomed me in two languages, and all the while the green-eyed man kept changing his tune.

Refugium

Now is the time to speak of narrow places," Sadie says. "Each of us can tell a story about a time they felt confined. And in this way, we commemorate the slavery of the Jews in Egypt."

"I have various questions," Maximiliano, Sadie's lover's fifteen-year-old son interrupts, holding up his hand like a traffic cop. "For who is the cup of wine at the end of the table, and why is the door open?"

Sadie had cleared a path down the central aisle of her used bookstore, emptied a display table, covered it in a blue tablecloth with orange birds along the hem. This long, makeshift table is now crowded with all the Passover accouterments. Her twin daughters, Little My and Mymble, yanked up jasmine from a neighbor's hedge and stuffed the vines in mugs. The delirious scent caresses the coalition squished shoulder to shoulder on benches and folding chairs.

Sadie's lover Daniel and his son Maximiliano, recently arrived from Chile, jostle each other on one side; Sadie, Little My and Mymble squish together across from them. All five are temporarily encamped in one room at the back of the bookstore, Daniel and Sadie on a foldout couch, Little My and Mymble on a blow-up mattress and Maximiliano on a cot, while they decide what to do next, and since Daniel and Maximiliano are on a three-month visa, they will need to decide soon.

Next to Sadie is her brother Isaac and next to Isaac, Lilah, the daughter he raised alone after his wife left. The ex-wife, Diane, and her partner Peyton have seats at the table, too. It's the first time Diane and Isaac have shared a meal since the divorce four years ago.

Everyone is walled in by stacks of displaced, used books. Everyone is three big glasses into the four required cups of wine. Mouths stained purple, Little My and Mymble are wildly giddy, partly from Manischewitz they've secretly mixed with their sparkling grape juice and partly from this outrageous winey secret.

"Good questions, Maximiliano," Sadie says now, her own lips wine-stained, her cheeks flushed. "Although there is a special time for questions at the Seder. Seder actually means 'order' in Hebrew."

"The full cup and the open door are for Elijah in case he stops by to tell us the messiah has arrived," Lilah tells Maximiliano. Lilah has a bony, beautiful face, wide shoulders, thick waist, narrow hips. She is substantial, Maximiliano is waif-like, skinny, leaning across the table toward Lilah like a dandelion in wind, his wild, dark hair a fluff about to seed.

"We're supposed to be telling stories," Little My says. "This isn't how it goes."

"Who wants to tell a story?" Sadie says. No one answers. "Okay, I'll go first. When our Grandfather Albert was a boy, his grandfather sat him on his lap and said, never forget you're a—"

Sadie is drowned out by a twin chorus of "Noo's." Mymble puts her head down gently on the table. Little My bangs her spoon. She says, "No, Mom, no. You are not telling that story again. It's not even a story. It's like a fact or a quote or something."

The sky outside is cerulean blue, orange-tinged, they can hear seals barking and an ambulance wailing away from them.

"Even I have heard that story more times than one," Daniel says gently.

"Whatevs," Sadie laughs, takes a gulp of wine. "Someone else go."

"It's not time to drink," Little My says.

"Little My," Daniel says, "why don't you go first. Give us the correct way."

Little My's real name is Sarah, but since she was five years old she has insisted on being called Little My, after a sly character in the Moomintroll books whose hair is always raked back in a vise-like ponytail. Little My wears her platinum blond hair in the same way. When her mother gathers her hair back every morning, she always demands, "Tighter, tighter." Sometimes the rubber band breaks. She wont let Daniel do it, says he doesn't pull tight enough. Ever since Little My named herself, Sadie began calling her other twin Mymble, after Little My's dreamier sister, so she would have a nickname, too. Mymble wears her dark brown hair in a ponytail, though not so tight.

"Why me?" Little My makes a stab at some charoses and stuffs it into her mouth.

"Because you've done this before," Sadie says. "This is Daniel and Maximiliano's first Passover. Show them how. And it's not time to eat yet."

"This charoses tastes wrong," Little My says, sticking her fork into Mymble's mouth so she can try.

"Yeah, hashtag ass," Mymble says.

"It's a Sephardic recipe," Diane says. "With cloves. Maybe too adventurous for this crowd."

"Hashtag ass is funny," Maximiliano grins.

"I'm sure the charoses is incredible," Sadie says. "Little My, please, a story."

"Like when I was stuck in Snufkin's pocket?" Little My says, and both girls crack up.

"That's Little My in the book. Mymble, what about you?"

Little My and Mymble's Story

"The time the monkey bars fell on Little My's head?" Mymble says.

"You told that last year!" Little My rolls her eyes.

"But Daniel and Maximiliano haven't heard it," Sadie says.

"What are monkey bars?" Maximiliano asks.

"A thing you play on," Little My says. She balances her soupspoon between two wine glasses. "Like this."

"Little My was on top of these giant metal monkey bars at Bierce Park," Mymble says. "They took them away after what happened because they are so dangerous."

"And I climbed up on the monkey bars, but Mymble was too afraid," Little My says. She sways her pointer finger as if it is balancing on the spoon.

"True," Mymble says. "I just stood there, like, no way, Jose. And suddenly the whole thing went wooooh, like ahhhh, and you should have seen Little My's face," Mymble laughs and so does Little My.

"Yeah I was like—" Little My makes her mouth and eyes into three O's.

"And it fell over and Little My fell off and bam it landed on Little My's head." Little My knocks the spoon off the glasses and wiggles her finger under it. "And Dad was supposed to be watching us but he was reading a book on the Once Upon a Time bench."

"I hate this part," Sadie says.

"No entiendo una mierda," Maximiliano says.

"But my head wasn't crushed because it fell in sand so my head sunk into the sand."

"But she looked crushed. Her eyes were closed and she wasn't saying anything."

"And then what happened?" Sadie smiles.

Mymble smiles and shrugs.

"What did you do?" Sadie says.

"Okay, okay, she saved me," Little My says. "She pulled the thing off my head like it was nothing. But later when everyone came to see what happened it took two adults to move the monkey bars." Little My bends Mymble's skinny arm, "Hidden muscles." Mymble keeps smiling.

"Was it really hard to lift?" Lilah asks.

"Pretty easy," Mymble says, "because my brother helped."

Little My shoots Mymble a hate look, and Mymble looks down at her plate, her smile stiff.

"Where's your brother?" It's the first thing Peyton has said.

"He died when we were born," Little My says.

"I've never heard this part about your brother helping," Sadie says. "You never said that."

Daniel reaches across and holds Sadie's hand. Isaac puts his arm around her shoulder.

155

"He's here right now," Mymble whispers, glancing at Little My defiantly. "He likes to sit between us."

"Can you see him?" Sadie asks.

"Mymble says she can," Little My says. "I used to be able to see him, but now I can just feel him."

"Can you see him, Mom?" Mymble asks.

"No," Sadie says. "But I can feel him. Just like I feel Grandpa Albert."

"Perhaps none of them are really gone. How beautiful, que lindo, no?" Daniel says. "What a perfect Passover story, as I understand it. The way out of the narrow place is imagination."

Little My grabs for some matzah.

Diane pulls the plate of matzah away. "You're going to get fat if you keep eating like that," she says.

"Jesus, Mom." Lilah hands Little My a whole matzah. "No need to screw Little My up, too."

"You tell a story, Daniel," Little My says, sharing her matzah with Mymble. She puts another piece of matzah on the table between herself and Mymble.

Daniel's Story

Daniel stares at the candlelight playing over his white plate, adjusts his blue yarmulke over his bald head, looks up and smiles at each person in turn. "This happened in Santiago de Chile when I was in university. I had a ponytail just like you girls. They called a general protest against Pinochet." He looks at Lilah. "Pinochet was a dictator—"

"I know who he was," Lilah says.

"He was a very bad man," Daniel says to the twins.

"Like the president," the girls say together.

"Don't even bring him up," Sadie says.

"How will that help?" Lilah asks.

"So," Daniel says. "My neighbor and I, we crept out after curfew. We filled a tire with gasoline to set on fire in the middle of the street. In this manner, when the police come, they couldn't get by, and everyone would know we are protesting for freedom. But the police came while we were still filling the tire with gasoline.

"We ran the block to return to the house. They were chasing us in the armored truck. In Santiago at that time I lived in the end of a small alley and at the front of the alley we have a gate. We were able to lock the gate, then we ran to the end of the alley, hoping to reach my house at the very end. The police officers pushed their guns in the bars of the gate and shoot a tear gas at the front window."

"Whoa," Mymble says.

"We ran into the house and kicked the can from the front door, but then they shoot another one in. My mother was in the house. Smoke was all over us. My neighbor and I knew tear gas, we held lemons on our noses and didn't rub our eyes."

"Lemons!" Little My says.

"Sí, this helps, but my mother never experienced it. She would not allow us to hold the lemon near to her face. She rubbed her burning eyes. She thought she can't breathe. She was choking and coughing, but we didn't dare to leave the house. We thought we would not escape that narrow place."

"I always think, why run home to your Mama's?" Maximiliano says.

Daniel smiles. "Forgive me. I was young, not much older than you."

Maximiliano shrugs. Takes a gulp of the wine.

"It's not time to drink yet," Little My says.

"Sorry," Maximiliano says.

Daniel looks at the children. "Perhaps the moral of this story is that once you emerge from your narrow place, you should not try to go back onto it."

"Into it," Little My corrects. "But what happened afterwards?"

"The police finally left. Mama was fine. The dictatorship ended. I escaped my narrow place, came to America, and after various adventures, here we all are, together."

"Congratulations, Sadie, it seems like you married your brother," Diane says.

"Jesus, Mom," Lilah says.

"What?" Diane says. "It was a compliment. Daniel and Isaac are both guys trying to make sure everything is always all right. Here's to all the people who don't mean any harm. Good for you."

Lilah turns away from her mother. "I really appreciate that story, Daniel, really," she says, "but since it's our tradition to talk about confinement and narrow places, how about what's happening right now, today, outside our personal, peaceful little circle. What about Syria? Or Palestine? Are we allowed to talk about Palestine?"

"Or the wall," Maximiliano says. "Are we not all trapped inside the great Gringolandia wall?"

"Excellent way of saying it," Lilah says.

"But, Lilah, you know we always talk about the plight of the Palestinians at Passover," Isaac says. "It just comes a little later in the Seder."

"Do you think the endless length of the Seder is meant to represent the Jews endless slavery in Egypt?" Lilah asks. Maximiliano laughs.

"If you're going to work for peace you have to start by respecting other people's traditions," Daniel says to Maximiliano.

Maximiliano switches to Spanish, hisses, "You're the one that's always going on and on about giving your life for peace and justice, and now you tell a story about what an incredible activist you were and saved Chile a million years ago, but what about now, today? What about the fact that you quit working for peace and justice and moved us to the evil empire? What about that?"

"We are in a transition moment," Daniel says in Spanish. "I will always work for world peace."

"Does fucking help world peace?" Maximiliano asks in English.

"Yes!" Daniel says.

Everyone else is quiet.

Peyton stands, raises her glass of wine. "I'm a poor white trash Asian-American orphan, so you can guess this is my first Passover." She has this Peter Pan half-smile on her face. "I've been a loner all my life, always lived by the motto: 'at a flies' picnic, how could you tell the guest flies from the regular, uninvited flies who just want to land on the food for a while?' So, no picnics for me. Diane and I moved into the middle of nowhere, no neighbors, which I like, but now suddenly Diane has decided she wants community. Like the woman's march for example, she recently insisted we participate in that.

And now here we are. L'chaim."

"The woman's march is really problematic," Lilah says. "It was just a bunch of white hetero ladies flouncing around with pussies on their heads and basically ignoring women of color and queer and trans people."

"We're queer and Peyton is a person of color," Diane says.

"Congratulations, Mom," Lilah says.

Isaac's Story

Isaac stands up. Like Sadie, Isaac has a long narrow nose, and like her, brown hair with sprigs of grey, and they're both beginning to grow easy in the tummy. "First off, I compliment the girls for putting jasmine on the table. In studies of the effect of the smell of jasmine on mice, they found that jasmine makes mice curl up in the corner of their cage and basically pass out. It acts like Valium on the senses. I have planted jasmine everywhere in my yard." He clears his throat. "So, I've been thinking about this idea of a refugium for months now. A refugium means an area in which a population of organisms can survive through a period of unfavorable conditions. At first, I was thinking about it mostly because I was building a greenhouse, but now I'm also thinking that this table, this group of people, in the current political climate, is like a refugium." There are murmurs of approval, glasses begin to raise, they think he's done, but he's not done.

"So, I was thinking, maybe this Passover we need to reverse our thinking. Sadie, I look at you, and even though you're living in one room with the boyfriend that deserted you years ago, just kicked you to the curb so to speak, the guy who has come crawling back and has no job and can't stay in this country."

"And has no hair," Little My says.

"And always wears the same blue shirt with a green stripe," Mymble says.

"He has three shirts the same," Maximiliano explains.

"So, for whatever reason you're giving him another chance, and you left your husband and you're living here in one room with three kids. I mean, that seems like the definition of a narrow place."

"I think we get the picture, Isaac," Sadie says.

"But look at you, you're radiant," Isaac continues. "Maybe you'll have to leave this country, so good, it's a good time to leave the country for a while. And your kids will have the adventure of a lifetime and maybe learn another language. Lilah wants to take care of the bookstore if you leave, by the way," he nods at Lilah. "She was going to talk to you today. Turn it into a bookstore café."

"An anarchist bookstore café and bicycle repair shop," Lilah says.

"Right." He tips his glass toward the other side of the table. "And Diane and her sensei, they seem okay. And I'm happy, too, believe it or not. I've discovered this passion for horticulture, for plants, and I've created my own magical forest hidden away in my apartment. In fact, right at this moment I'm worrying about them, hoping they're okay without me, is the temperature right, the humidity, are they hydrated, that kind of thing. What I'm saying is that in a way, for all of us, happily ever after has turned out to be a narrow place."

"Bravo," Daniel says.

"I kind of feel like I'm in the opposite of a narrow place," Sadie says.

"So, Dad, you're celebrating the bubble you've made through your own privilege to protect you from the real, actual danger so many people are in because of this administration?" Lilah asks.

"For once I agree with my daughter," Diane says. "That's what I meant about Daniel and Isaac being basically the same guy. Here we are in the middle of the apocalypse, and they are both assuring us we've never been happier."

Isaac flings his wine at Diane.

The wine rorschachs across her expensive looking, oversized, beige sweater with the wide neck.

Everyone goes silent.

"This is an unfavorable condition," Diane says, pushing back her expensively highlighted hair. "Covered in cheap wine."

Peyton says, "I thought you were all hot for community, Di."

Diane nods, takes a deep breath, grips the table. "I actually have a good bottle of wine hidden here in my bag. I was only sharing it with Peyton. I'm sorry." She wrestles the bottle out of her giant beige leather bag. She stands, a little wobbly, Manischewitz dripping like syrup down her sweater. She knocks some books over as she edges around the table. She fills Isaac's cup right to the brim, then she fills Lilah's cup. She hugs Isaac's head against her. She grabs Lilah's hand and squeezes, and Lilah lets her. "Thanks for inviting us, both of you."

Isaac wipes wine off the side of his head. "I can get that out. With cold water and salt," he says.

Peyton helps Diane pull off her sweater and hands it to Isaac. He goes to the back sink behind the counter. The water turns on. Diane looks small in her small white t-shirt.

"I have a story," Lilah says. "Remember that old white guy Mr. Nowicki who disappeared and his house burnt down and all that? So, this homeless guy I met yesterday told me that another homeless guy told him that he saw Mr. Nowicki and that writer—that Asian guy—"

"Dave Tanaka," Sadie and Diane say at the same time.

Peyton sips her wine.

"Yeah, Dave Tanaka. Anyway, he saw the two of them together in a beat-up old RV in the Adirondacks, camped out by a stream. They were sitting in folding chairs, fishing and drinking cocktails, but the writer had propped his fishing pole against his chair and was trying to write on his laptop and the old guy kept telling him to watch his line, and the writer said leave me alone I'm writing."

"That is very possibly a true story," Peyton says.

"Where did you hear that?" Diane asks.

"From this homeless guy Maximiliano and I met, right Maxi?"

Maximiliano mumbles something into his plate that ends in "deer."

"What's this about a deer?" Daniel says.

"There was a deer," Maximiliano says. "Yesterday."

"Is this your Seder story?" Little My asks. "Because Uncle Isaac just basically gave a speech."

Maximiliano and Lilah's Story

"It's this deer, yes? Yesterday, Papa says to me, Stop playing video games immediately and go to the woods. Then, suddenly my new cousin, Lilah is in the room to go with me to the woods. Lilah, you continue the story."

"Sure," Lilah laughs. "At first we were both totally bummed to be stuck together."

"Si seguro, my son was very angry we force him to walk in the forest with a beautiful older woman."

"I was no angry, only timid," Maximiliano nods.

"So, we walked to San Buenaventura, and we ended up having this great conversation, we really connect on a lot of things, and we were just talking and walking up into this gorge, like a long way up, up by the falls, and no one else was there because it was like weirdly grey and cold yesterday, remember? And we stumbled on this tent set up under the falls. It was a sweet site for a camp. A homeless guy was living there. We started talking."

"Scary story," Mymble says, climbing onto Sadie's lap.

"But it is a story," Little My says.

Isaac comes back into the room holding a box of kosher salt. "This was yesterday?"

"So, he was telling us about his life and we were just talking about kind of deep things. Then we saw this deer. It was tiptoeing along the cliff edge above the falls. When we saw it we were all, Whoa, holy shit! The deer heard us and freaked. It tried to turn around on the ledge or whatever. And it fell off the cliff. Like a long way."

"Are you serious?" Diane says. "I thought deer were

sure-footed, like cats."

"It was lying half in this pool at the bottom of the falls and half on the like, gravel," Lilah says. "Its back was broken or something. It couldn't move even when we got up close to it, except it's eyes were rolling around. We realized if we left it there, the coyotes or dogs would get it."

"Did you call the cops?" Little My asks.

"We put it out of misery," Maximiliano says. "That's what Chris calls it."

"The homeless guy was named Chris," Lilah says.

"Coño," Daniel says. "This is yesterday?"

"You didn't tell me this, Lilah," Isaac says. "What do you mean you put it out of its misery?"

"Chris was like, 'We have to put this deer out of its misery.' And he handed Maximiliano a big rock," Lilah says.

"Jesus," Isaac says, thumping down the salt.

"You should have taken it to the vet," Mymble says.

"I was not able to do this misery," Maximiliano says. "I give the rock to Lilah."

"I couldn't do it, either. I just stood there holding the rock while the deer silently struggled. Finally, Chris took the rock and hit it, but it wouldn't die, so he hit it really hard, with both hands above his head, like five times. He was, like, foaming at the mouth. Chris."

Diane pulls Little My onto her lap. She doesn't struggle. Isaac comes and stands behind Lilah and puts his hands on her shoulders.

Maximiliano looks at Lilah.

Nobody says anything. Then Daniel squeezes Maximiliano's forearm. "That's an excellent Passover story," he says.

Maximiliano's eyes dart over to Daniel.

Diane laughs like a surprised bark.

"No, in truth, I am not jesting, so many narrow places—for each one in the story, the deer, the man, the girl, the boy. It's a wonderful metaphor."

The little bell on the door jingles.

"We're closed," Sadie calls.

"Daniel, meet your metaphor," Lilah says.

A man stands in the doorway. He has dark hair cut into blunt bangs and cut bluntly at his shoulders. He has a port-wine stain birthmark that washes down one side of his face and swells his lips on that side. He's wearing a small, dirty UC Santa Cruz slug sweatshirt. His long wrists and hands hang out of the tight sweatshirt, very thin and raw looking. He brings with him a strong, complicated yeasty smell. "Hi, folks," he says.

"This is him. The man we meet in the woods. Chris. We invite him to the party."

"I know you," Diane says. "We haven't been formally introduced, but I've seen you at the dumpster at my restaurant. Diane's."

"Best dumpster in town," Chris says.

"Thank you."

"I used to hear you at the park," Sadie says. "I mean, see you."

"It's okay, he knows they call him Señor Screamer," Lilah says.

"I never understood that—Señor. I always scream in English," he says. "I have a condition. It's not something I can control. But I don't scream at the park anymore, it turns out it really bothered people. Like you," Chris

166

says to Peyton. "You're the lady that attacked me in the park."

"I don't like loud noises," Peyton says.

"She spent her childhood hidden in the stacks of a library," Diane says.

"Could you teach me how to do that?" Chris says. "That karate chop thing to the throat?"

"Probably not," Peyton says.

"Please, Chris, sit down," Sadie says. "We're just finishing up the Seder. In fact, it's probably time to eat."

"We didn't sing 'Dayenu,'" Little My says.

Chris knocks some books over as he edges to sit in Elijah's seat. He pushes the cup of wine away. "I don't drink," he says.

Lilah pours him some sparkling grape juice.

"Okay, okay, 'Dayenu,'" Sadie says. "Dayenu means 'enough.' Ilu hotzi, hotzi anu Hotzi anu mi mitzrayim," Sadie begins to sing. Others join in. Sadie picks up the scallion by her plate and hits Mymble on the head with it. "Everyone join in! Mi mitzrayim, hotzi anu, Dayenu!" Little My takes up her scallion and smacks Maximiliano on the cheek.

"Chucha," Maximiliano swears.

"It's part of the Seder," Mymble says.

Maximiliano grins and smacks Lilah with his scallion. She smacks back.

"Ilu hotzi, hotzi anu," Sadie sings, and everyone joins in or mumbles along and smacks each other with scallions.

"Too violent," Chris comments.

Maximiliano whips Sadie on the back of the neck.

Daniel sings, "Day-e-nu" and scallions Diane

smartly on the forehead, once for each syllable.

Chris begins to scream.

Little My and Mymble stand on either side of Peyton and take turns bopping her on the head.

At first everyone continues smacking and singing, but the yelling grows more full-throated, larger, and the scallions droop, and everyone turns to look at Chris. He's screaming, "Mothhher Fuuucker" and "Cock Sucker" and "Cunnilingus ass-wipe."

Chris's eyes are large and frightened, as if he is signaling for help with them.

"Do you want a glass of water?" Sadie asks him.

He screams, "Fuuuck you, you green bitch."

"Try to breathe," Isaac suggests.

"Anus, bad breath, hot potato," Chris screams.

Peyton's hands begin to rise. "I don't like loud noises," she says.

Mymble presses her hands over Peyton's ears. Little My covers Mymbles hands on Peyton's ears. They stand like that, hands over each other's hands over Peyton's ears, their faces very close, whispering their hot breath secrets that only they and Peyton can hear. Peyton smiles that killer smile.

Maximiliano gives Lilah an anarchist salute, bent arm, closed fist. Lilah dances two fingers over one eye, two fingers over the other back at him.

Chris screams, "Piss Ant, Gerrymandering, Fuck Sauce."

"And I thought you were going to be the one to F'up Passover, Diane," Sadie smiles.

Diane rolls her eyes and smiles back.

Daniel claps his hands, says, "This is it, yes, a pure

outpouring of feeling, yes!"

Sadie says, "Daniel, give the narration a rest." She notices that the matzah between Little My and Mymble is gone. "Who wants matzah ball soup?" she says.

"I Want A Fucking Matzah Ball Please," Chris screams.

Isaac mumbles, "This is why I like plants," and knocks his chair over as he stands. He heads for the door.

Lilah calls, "Dad, come back!"

A siren screams towards them.

Chris screams.

Isaac presses his hands to his ears. "I choose plants."

"Isaac," Sadie says, "we're about to have soup."

Acknowledgments

My gratitude to the magazines and anthologies who published the following stories in different forms: "King of Chains," *Catamaran Literary Reader,* 2014; republished in *Saturday Evening Post* and *California Prose Directory*, Outpost19 in 2015; audio book on Audible, Spring, 2016; "Quiero Bailar Slow With You Tonight," *ZYZZYVA*, Spring, 2004; "There once was a woman who longed for a child" as "Happily Ever After" in *Red Wheel Barrow*, Volume 11, 2010; "The Comeback Tour," *Chicago Quarterly Review*, Winter, 2011; "We Are The Same People," *Massachusetts Review*, 2004 and the anthology *The Best Underground Fiction*, Volume One, Stolen Time Publishing, 2005; "To My Best Friend Who Hates Me," *Columbia*, Issue #39, 2004; "Miraculous Escapes by Dave Tanaka" as "Treasure Island," *Santa Cruz Noir*, Akashic Press, Summer, 2018; "Back at the Beginning, Dangerously Close to the End" as "Occurrence at Aquidneck Island," *Encyclopedia,* Summer, 2017; "There Once Was A Man Who Longed For A Child," *Joyland*, and as an audio book on Audible, 2016 and in *Golden State 2017: Best New Fiction and Nonfiction from California*, Outpost19, Spring 2017; "Refugium" as "Ghost Deer," Winner, Machigonne Fiction Contest, *New Guard*, Volume four, Spring, 2015; "Breathing Room" in *Epoch*, 2001.

I'm so grateful for my residency at the Blue Mountain Center, especially to Directors Harriet Barlow and Ben Strader, as well as for support from the University of California, Santa Cruz; forever gratitude to the following astute and generous readers: Jill Wolfson, Melissa Sanders-Self, Kathy Chetkovich, Karen Tei Yamashita, Samson Stilwell, Esther Stilwell, Naomi Tannen, Joe Mahay, Kim Lau, Juan Poblete, Susie Bright, Molly Antopol, Lisa McKenzie and Karen Joy Fowler; Zöe Ruiz, publicist extraordinaire; Jon Roemer, thank you for pushing me forward, for honesty, for support; and Juan, no matter what shirt you wear, always, always.

about Micah Perks

Micah Perks is the author of the novel *What Becomes Us*, winner of an Independent Publisher's Book Award and named one of the Top Ten Books about the Apocalypse by *The Guardian*. Her memoir, *Pagan Time*, tells the story of her childhood in a log cabin on a commune in the Adirondack wilderness. She is also the author of *We Are Gathered Here*, a novel, and Alone in the Woods, a long personal essay. Her short stories and essays have appeared in *Epoch, Zyzzyva, Tin House, The Toast, OZY* and *The Rumpus*, amongst many journals and anthologies. She has won an NEA, five Pushcart Prize nominations, and the New Guard Machigonne 2014 Fiction Prize. She received her BA and MFA from Cornell University and now lives with her family in Santa Cruz where she co-directs the creative writing program at UCSC. More info and work at micahperks.com